Phoebe finds her feet

Kathy Lee

Other books in the Phoebe series:

Fabulous Phoebe
Phoebe's Fortune
Phoebe's Book of Body Image, Boys and Bible Bits

Also by the same author:

Deadly Emily
Flood Alert!
Seasiders: Runners
Seasiders: Liar
Seasiders: Joker
Seasiders: Winner
Seasiders: Angels

Copyright © Kathy Lee 2003
First published 2003, reprinted 2005
ISBN 1 85999 701 5

Scripture Union, 207–209 Queensway, Bletchley, Milton Keynes, MK2 2EB, England.

Email: info@scriptureunion.org.uk
Website: www.scriptureunion.org.uk

Scripture Union Australia
Locked Bag 2, Central Coast Business Centre, NSW 2252
Website: www.su.org.au

Scripture Union USA
PO Box 987, Valley Forge, PA 19482
www.scriptureunion.org

British Library Cataloguing-in-Publication Data.

A catalogue record of this book is available from the British Library.

Printed and bound in Great Britain by Creative Print and Design (Wales) Ebbw Vale.

Cover design: PRE Consultants Ltd

℘ Scripture Union is an international Christian charity working with churches in more than 130 countries, providing resources to bring the good news about Jesus Christ to children, young people and families and to encourage them to develop spiritually through the Bible and prayer.

As well as our network of volunteers, staff and associates who run holidays, church-based events and school Christian groups, we produce a wide range of publications and support those who use our resources through training programmes.

Contents

Chapter One

The French exchange part 1

"I wonder what she'll be like?" I said for about the fiftieth time.

"I wish you'd stop saying that," said Ellie, my best friend. "You know exactly what she'll be like. French... age 14... called Julie."

"Not Julie. Shoo-*lee*," I said, trying to say it the way the French teacher did. Ellie fell about laughing.

"What's so funny?"

"Just for a second then, you looked exactly like Mrs Cole."

"Oh, thanks a bunch."

Mrs Cole, the Head of French, is fat and 50ish, with orange hair and a permanent scowl. (She's the main reason why eighty per cent of Year 10 chose to do German.) I don't think I look anything like her. Apart from being fat, that is.

What do I look like? If I could score points for various bits of my appearance, I'd probably get 7 out of 10 for my face, and 9 out of 10 for my hair, which is long and blonde. My figure would rate about 1 out of 10.

Maybe I shouldn't go around with Ellie, who is tall and slim and makes me look even fatter than I am. But we've been friends since infant school. We're both easy to spot in the Reception class photo – Ellie is the tallest kid in the class and I'm the fattest. The photographer banished us to the back row, along with Hugh (enormous ears) and Joey (no front teeth). Ten years on, things haven't changed much. Ellie is still taller than most of the boys in our year, and I'm still fatter than all of them. Needless to say, neither of us has a boyfriend.

It was the week of the French exchange. Fifty French pupils would soon be arriving in Sandersfield to stay with Year 10 students. Next term we would make a return visit to their school on the outskirts of Paris.

"You are lucky, getting a boy," I said to Ellie.

"Don't say that until you've met him," she said. "He's probably a cross-eyed midget with breath that stinks of garlic."

"I didn't know the Hunchback of Notre Dame was going on the French exchange... nobody tells me anything."

Because there were not enough English boys involved in the exchange, a few French boys had been paired with English girls. Ellie's one was called Pierre. It was quite likely that he would be a midget compared to Ellie. As for garlic breath, we would have to wait and see.

Naturally, I would have preferred to have a boy to stay, but we didn't have a spare bedroom. I share a room with my sister Georgie, who was moving in with my little brother Josh so that the French girl could use her bed. Georgie was *not* happy about this.

What would the French girl think of our house? What would she think of the bedroom, still crowded with Georgie's possessions, such as dozens of fluffy toys, three elderly Barbie dolls and a kids' karaoke system?

Not to mention:

- Mum's cooking (cordon bleuugghh).
- Dad's attempts at French (highly embarrassing).
- my own attempts (even more embarrassing).
- Josh's attempts at English (mega, mega embarrassing – lots of toilet words).

- my taste in clothes, make-up, music, films, etc.
- the delights of my home town (Paris compared to Sandersfield is like a gourmet meal compared to a bag of cold chips).

In fact I was dreading the French exchange. I wished I had never agreed to take part in it. What I needed was a sudden attack of some dreadful disease… typhoid or TB. Or else the house could be severely damaged by a gas explosion. Or ferocious storms could prevent all ferries from crossing the Channel…

"Oh, come on, Phoebe," said Ellie. "It can't possibly be that bad. Even if it is, they'll only be here for a week."

It was going to be a long week. Somehow I just knew it.

The French mob were due to arrive on Wednesday evening. Dad took me to school to collect Julie and her luggage. The coach was late, so we hung around in the school hall, trying not to look nervous.

Venice, another friend of mine, came over to us. She said, "Are you having a girl or a boy?"

"Sounds like I'm pregnant," I said, and Dad gave me a startled look. (He always pretends not to listen in when I'm talking to friends, but now and then I catch him out.) "It's a girl. How about you?"

"Mine's called Michel."

"Is that male or female?" I asked, but Venice wasn't sure. "Didn't old Coleface tell you?"

"I don't think so… I can't remember."

Venice didn't seem at all worried about the exchange. But then whoever she got, boy, girl or Hunchback of Notre Dame, would probably be impressed by Venice's home, which was enormous. Venice's mum used to be a famous model. (Not that you would guess by looking at Venice, who is quite ordinary-looking, with mouse-brown hair and a nose too long for her face.)

"The coach is here!" someone called, and everyone moved towards the windows. Outside, the French pupils were getting out of the coach as the driver unloaded their luggage. Without hearing them speak, you wouldn't have guessed they were from a foreign country. They wore the same kind of clothes, and even the same designer labels, as we did.

"Mmm. He looks OK," Venice muttered, pointing to a tall, dark guy in a leather jacket.

"That's a teacher, you idiot."

"So? Is there some law that says you can't fancy teachers?"

I was more interested in looking at the girls, wondering which one was Julie. Please, not that one with the three matching suitcases. (Three suitcases! For a week!) And not that slim, tall, beautiful girl, straight off a magazine cover. It would be better if Julie was the smiling red-haired girl, or even the shy one standing all alone...

Mrs Cole began directing the French pupils into the hall, where they were matched up with their host families. The mysterious Michel turned out to be male and rather good-looking. Venice looked smug as she led him away.

Across the room, I saw Ellie being introduced to a small boy in glasses. She made a despairing face at me over the top of his head.

The crowd was thinning. Outside, the last few visitors collected their luggage, leaving only one – the pretty girl I'd noticed before. She seemed angry. Her dark eyes flashed with temper. She shook her head, and her black hair rippled like a storm-tossed flag. (How is it that some people still look good even when they're in a foul mood?) She was arguing with the coach driver, who shrugged his shoulders as if to say, *not my problem*.

"What's all that about?" I asked Dad.

His French is marginally better than mine (not difficult). He said, "Sounds like her suitcase has gone missing."

I hate to admit this, but just for a second I felt pleased. Beautiful people seem to glide through life like swans, admired by everyone. They don't like it when problems ruffle the smooth surface of their lives. Well, all I can say is – tough.

By now the girl was making a huge fuss. Two French teachers got drawn into it, along with Mrs Cole. I looked around, and my heart sank. The hall was emptying as the other French kids went off with their host families. Only Dad and I were left... which meant the girl outside must be Julie.

Mrs Cole strode in, scowling even worse than usual. "Oh, there you are, Phoebe. That's your exchange student outside. She's lost her bag."

"How did she manage that?" asked Dad.

"Apparently the coach had to stop outside Calais because a boy needed his asthma inhaler. It was in his suitcase in the luggage compartment. How about that for planning and forethought? They had to unload half the cases and then reload them in a hurry so as not to miss the ferry. They think that's when it went missing."

"Was there anything valuable in it?"

"No actual money, fortunately, but all her clothes and things. She only has what she's wearing now. Perhaps Phoebe could lend..." Her voice tailed off.

I knew why. All my clothes would be about six sizes

too big for Julie. She looked slim enough to fit into Georgie's things – if she didn't mind wearing lime green crop tops and boy-band T-shirts.

"Anyway, come and meet the girl." Mrs Cole led us outside, where the argument was still raging in a torrent of fast-flowing French. Julie pointed down the road, as if she expected the coach driver to set off immediately back to Dover and across the Channel. One French teacher was trying to calm her down; the other was talking on a mobile.

Mrs Cole barged in and introduced us. I tried to think of something to say in French, but my mind was suddenly as empty as an old crisp packet.

Julie looked me up and down. She didn't seem impressed. I read somewhere that people decide whether they like you or not within 15 seconds of meeting you – before you have the chance to say anything.

To fill the awkward silence, Dad said, "Sorry to hear about your lost suitcase. But don't worry, Phoebe can lend you some things."

I wished he hadn't said that. For an instant Julie looked quite horrified. (Not only would my clothes go around her twice, I bet she wouldn't be seen dead in them anyway.) Then her face went all smooth and polite. "You are very kind," she said, attempting to smile.

Only a week, I reminded myself. Only 168 hours. And time really flies when you're enjoying yourself.

Chapter Two

Language problems

"Well, I'm sure you want to get home," said Mrs Cole. "Monsieur Duval is doing everything possible to track down that case." She steered us firmly in the direction of the car park, then headed back to talk to the French teachers.

If Venice or Ellie had been there, I would have said, "Old Cole fancies that French teacher. Hope he manages to escape in time." But I couldn't say that sort of thing to Julie. Not in French, at any rate – my French wasn't up to it.

I racked my brain for something to say as we drove home. We had been taught a few useful phrases, but none of them seemed tactful just then. *Did you have a good journey? Would you like to unpack your things? Do you like England?* Looking at Julie's sullen face, I was pretty sure each of those would get a one-word answer.

I suddenly realised how much I depend on words. By talking to people and making them laugh, I can show them I'm not just a fat lump of lard. I do have a sense of humour... it might be worth getting to know me.

Somehow I didn't think this was going to help me with Julie – unless her English was a lot better than my French. Still, it was worth a try.

We were driving along the High Street, which is all estate agencies, hair salons and flea-bitten charity shops. I said, "This is the centre of town. The Champs-Elysees of Sandersfield. How does it compare with Paris?"

I had to say it twice before she understood. By then I

was wishing I hadn't bothered. Especially when Julie said, as if explaining to a 6-year-old, "Paris is bigger. Paris has many shops."

Really? You don't say! I relapsed into silence.

Things went slightly better when we got home. My mum may not be a cordon bleu cook, and she has forgotten any French she ever knew, but she *is* good at making people feel welcome. When she heard about Julie's lost luggage, she was full of sympathy.

"Would you like to phone any of your friends, Julie? Perhaps they could lend you some clothes, or we could ask Phoebe's friend Ellie. She's tall and slim, like you. Don't worry. You won't have to wear the same clothes for a whole week."

Julie looked grateful. I had thought she was stupid to make such a fuss about her suitcase. Totally over-reacting! But maybe I would feel just as bad if I arrived in France with nothing but my passport and a half-eaten packed lunch.

"Come and eat," said Mum. "You must be hungry after your journey."

Hungry or not, Julie didn't eat much toad-in-the-hole or apple pie. Didn't she like foreign food? Or was she one of those people who stayed slim by eating almost nothing? Whichever, she gave me a disapproving look as I took a second helping of apple pie.

As soon as we'd finished, she was on the phone to her friends. (Luckily we had been given a list of host names and addresses.) Dad offered to drive her to the various places where people had spare clothes to lend. "You come too," he said to me.

"Do I have to?" I muttered.

"She *is* your guest."

Yeah.

But it was pointless, me being there. At the first house we visited, Julie and her friend vanished upstairs, gabbling in French. I was left on the doorstep. After a while I went slowly back to the car.

"What's the matter?" asked Dad.

"I dunno. I just don't think we're going to get on, Julie and me."

"Why? Because of the language barrier?"

"Well, that doesn't help. But I don't think she would like me even if I spoke perfect French."

Dad said, "Give the girl a chance, Phoebe. She's upset about losing her things. Once she's got over that, she might be a completely different person."

He was being all calm and logical, which didn't help. I wanted sympathy, not calmness and logic. Men! Mum would have understood exactly how I felt.

We spent most of the evening parked outside various houses. Soon Julie had quite a collection of things in the bag we had lent her. Most importantly, she now had clothes for the party which would be held at the school the following night. (The girl with three suitcases had packed four different party outfits.)

"That's great," said Dad. "Do you need anything else?"

Julie said, "The shoes. It's difficult… I have the large feet."

"What size?" I asked.

"*Quarante-trois*. That is, er… 43."

"What?" I looked down at her feet, wondering how I'd managed not to notice these monstrosities. But they looked (for Julie's height) quite normal.

"Continental sizes are different from ours," said Dad. "Would Ellie have anything, do you think?"

I rang her. Ellie discovered, by looking inside some trainers, that 43 was the same as her own size 9. Yes, she would be quite happy to lend Julie some shoes for the party.

"How's it going with Pierre?" I asked.

"Not wonderful," Ellie said guardedly. "We've got cat problems. You'll see when you come around."

Cat problems? Was Pierre afraid of them, or allergic, or something? Ellie was very fond of Casper, her gorgeous grey Persian cat. If Pierre didn't get on with Casper, he would lose about a million brownie points.

Even before Ellie answered the door, I could hear Casper mewing loudly.

"We've had to shut him in the kitchen," said Ellie, looking gloomy. "And Mum's had to vacuum the entire house. Apparently Pierre has bad asthma, and cats make it even worse."

"But why didn't he tell anybody?"

"He says he wrote it down on the application form. Mrs Cole can't have noticed. I mean, she never asked me anything about cats."

Oh, great. How about that for planning and forethought, eh, Mrs Cole?

Pierre was in the living room, watching TV. He said hello in a breathless voice. I could hear his wheezy breathing from right across the room.

As soon as Julie saw him, she said something mean to him in French. (I couldn't translate a word of it, but I could understand the tone of her voice all right. And the hurt look on Pierre's face.)

"Come on, let's look at some shoes," Ellie said hurriedly, leading us upstairs to her room. While Julie tried on shoes, Ellie asked her how she had come to lose her suitcase.

Julie said angrily, "It is Pierre. Because he has not his..." She couldn't think of the right word.

"Inhaler?" I suggested.

"Yes. He should have his inhaler with him. Then the coach does not stop and I don't lose my bag." She smiled a nasty little smile. "*C'est bien*. It's good that he is ill. I am happy."

She might have meant it as a joke... but somehow I didn't think so.

Next day in school, Ellie and I both had a good moan. (The French students had been whisked off to London in their coach. They were going to visit the Globe Theatre, the Tower, the London Eye, etc.)

"Pierre wouldn't be too bad, if it wasn't for his asthma," said Ellie. "But poor old Casper! He can't stand being shut in the kitchen – he'll go mad by the end of the week. And so will Mum. She was up early this morning, hoovering madly."

"Did it help at all?" I asked.

"I don't think so. Pierre sounded really wheezy at breakfast. Still, maybe a day out in London will make him feel better."

"With a bit of luck," I said, "he'll forget his inhaler again. They'll stop the coach to look for it, and Julie will get left behind and I'll never see her again."

"I don't see why you've got it in for Julie. She seems OK to me. Why do you hate her so much?"

"Because *she* hates *me*," I said. "She took one look at me and decided she didn't like me."

Actually, a small inner voice reminded me, that's not strictly true. You disliked her before she ever saw you. Because she's pretty and slim and confident-looking, you disliked her on sight.

Trying to ignore this thought, I said, "And you heard how mean she was about Pierre."

"Huh! He deserves it."

I was starting to feel a bit guilty. The thing is, I'm a Christian, and Christians are not supposed to hate people. 'Love your enemies, do good to those who hate you', it says in the Bible.

Do good to those who hate you... so I shouldn't really be bitching about Julie behind her back, should I? I ought to forget that bad first impression, and do my best to make friends.

I tried to do it – I really tried. That evening, as we got ready for the party, I made several attempts to be sociable. I asked her about the trip to London. ("It was interesting," she said in a flat voice that suggested total boredom.) I lent her some of my make-up, although she didn't think much of it. I warned her about Sean and Jake, who think of themselves as the super-studs of Year 10. She gave me a condescending smile.

"You do not have a boyfriend, Phoebe?"

I shook my head.

"You never had a boyfriend."

"Er... no. Have you got one?"

"*Mais, oui.* Naturally."

I resented her assumption that no boy would ever be desperate enough to ask me out. But I struggled to keep things polite. "What's he like, your boyfriend?"

"His name is Michel. He goes to the party tonight."

So much for Venice's chances! Oh well, there was always Monsieur Duval...

"Is he nice?"

She gave me a suspicious look. "*Pourquoi?* Why is it that you ask?"

End of conversation.

I was tired of trying to be friendly and getting nothing back. We finished getting ready in silence.

Chapter Three

The jealous type

The party was held in the school gym. It had been decorated with a few French and English flags, which couldn't disguise the peeling paintwork or the smell of sweaty trainers.

Although the French students arrived with their hosts, pretty soon French and English had separated into two groups, like oil and vinegar forming two distinct layers. This was only natural – but Mrs Cole had plans to mix us all up again.

For this was to be no ordinary school dance. It had a theme: Dancing Through the Ages. To begin, there was a performance by the local Morris Men. The French kids watched and applauded politely. They probably wondered why grown men should behave like this – waving hankies, hitting sticks together, and skipping about with bells on, all the time looking intensely serious.

"At least it keeps them off the streets and out of trouble," I muttered to Ellie.

Venice arrived. "Look, that's Michel over there," she said. "Nice, don't you think?"

"He's already got a girlfriend," I warned her, just as Julie draped herself around him like a boa constrictor. Venice looked bitterly disappointed.

The Morris dancers went off, jingling and jangling. Miss Marne, the Games teacher, appeared with a microphone and a sudden blast of country dance music.

I said, "Time for a quick trip to the loo. Or even a

slow trip – this might have finished by the time we get back."

But it hadn't. Miss Marne was calling out instructions for something called the Gay Gordons, and Mrs Cole was translating into French. The result was complete chaos on the dance floor. Couples were going forwards, backwards and sideways, all at the same time.

I noticed Pierre sitting at a side table, looking rather lonely. I nudged Ellie. "You ought to be looking after your guest. Go and talk to him."

Before she could tell me to get lost, a French boy asked her to dance. Rather than sit by myself, I went to talk to Pierre.

"How's your asthma?"

"It's better because I am far from the cat." He gave me a shy smile. "I don't like the dancing, but I hope it will continue for a long time. Then I must go back and meet my enemy."

Wow! He had said more in 30 seconds than Julie had in an entire day. "Your English is very good," I said admiringly.

"You think so? It's because I have lived in England. I went to school in Richmond for one year, when my father was working in London. So I had to learn very quickly to speak English."

"How old were you at the time?" I asked him.

"8 years old. When you are younger it's easier to learn, I think. But I have forgotten very much."

That smile again… If he didn't have to wear those thick glasses, and wasn't so small, he could be quite interesting. He was a Grade C. (C = Could be OK, if …)

His breathing still sounded slightly wheezy, though much better than the day before. "You know, you should tell your teachers about the cat," I said. "They might be able to move you to a house with no pets."

"I have told Monsieur Duval, but he says he can't do anything. He thinks I am a... a nuisance. Because of me, because of the asthma, the coach was late and Julie lost her baggage." He looked miserable.

"But that's so unfair! You can't help having asthma. And it's not your fault you were put in a house with a cat. You can blame our French teacher for that. She's such a—"

A hand descended on my shoulder. "Phoebe!" Mrs Cole bellowed in my ear. "Don't sit on the sidelines, we need people on the dance floor. Up you get!"

She practically dragged Pierre and me out of our seats. Then she went on around the room, bullying and threatening, until the dance floor was full again.

I felt embarrassed. Pierre had said he hated dancing, but he had been too polite to refuse. He would never have asked me to dance – not me, big fat Phoebe, two inches taller and three stone heavier than he was.

"The next dance," Miss Marne boomed, "will be a progressive one. As the dance repeats, the boys stay in the same place and the girls move on to new partners."

Oh well, Pierre wouldn't have to put up with me for long... We learned the moves, the music started, and we were off.

To my surprise I quite enjoyed it. As we swapped partners, I danced with several boys who never normally noticed me. (And I can tell you, Sean Miles may be good-looking, but he's a useless dancer.) As the music stopped, who should I end up with but Michel? Now that I saw him close up it was easy to understand why Venice liked him.

"Don't move! Keep your partners for the next dance!" Miss Marne shouted.

Michel looked down at me. He had very intense, deep blue eyes. "What is your name?"

"Phoebe."

"Phoebe," he murmured. "What a beautiful name."

I have this problem – I blush very easily. There's nothing I can do about it once it starts. I just have to ignore it and hope that people don't notice.

"You're called Michel, aren't you?" I said.

"Yes. How do you know this?"

"My friend told me."

Michel didn't look surprised. He smiled, as if he rather expected girls to talk about him all the time. I glanced up and caught Julie staring at me. She didn't look at all happy that I was talking to her boyfriend and getting ready to dance with him.

The dance was called the St Bernard's Waltz. It meant Michel had to hold me quite close, and I felt myself starting to blush again, especially when he stroked my hair. As Julie twirled past us in the dance, I saw her face was like thunder.

At the end of the dance, Michel thanked me politely and we parted company. I felt rather hot, so Ellie, Venice and I grabbed some Cokes from the bar and went outside for a breather. We weren't the only ones. Quite a few people were lurking in dark corners, having a quick smoke/snog/illegal can of lager.

We debated whether French boys were nicer than English ones. Ellie said they were more romantic.

"Yes," said Venice. "When I told Michel my name, he said, 'Venice. What a beautiful name.' I mean, no way would an English boy say that."

I laughed. "He said exactly the same to me. I think he's a bit too smooth... not to say slippery."

Hints for English boys: how to act romantic:

(NB It helps if you are tall, dark and handsome, with Mediterranean suntan.)

1 Make the girl feel really special.
2 Tell her something nice about herself.
   (Ermintrude... what a beautiful name.)
3 Speak with an intriguing foreign accent.
4 Look deeply into her eyes.
5 Touch her gently in a non-threatening way.
6 Ask her out to see a romantic film. (This means one with no fights, car chases, alien monsters or sick jokes. Sorry, boys.)
7 Send her a huge sentimental Valentine card.
8 If no response, forget her – she's not the romantic type. Find another girl and start again at 1.

When we went back in, there were noticeably fewer people in the gym, and more than half of them were female. Mrs Cole press-ganged every available male onto the dance floor, leaving a few spare girls, including me (surprise, surprise).

"The next dance will be a Ladies' Excuse Me," Miss Marne announced. "Girls, if you don't have a partner, you are allowed to tap another girl on the shoulder, say 'Excuse me', and take her partner."

Oh, the fun they must have had in the days before TV. It's amazing they didn't die from the excitement.

As the dance got under way, Mrs Cole prowled around the edge of it, encouraging the extra girls to join in. "Come on, it's easy! Just step in and say 'Excuse me' – like this!"

She tapped the nearest passing girl and slid into the

arms of her partner, who happened to be Michel. (Interesting – he hadn't been dancing with Julie.) Michel shot me a look of mock dismay, followed by one of real agony as Mrs Cole stood on his foot.

When the circling dance took them past me again, they were still together. Over Mrs Cole's bright orange head, Michel looked at me pleadingly. What else could I do? I stepped forward and said "Excuse me" to Mrs Cole.

"Thank you," Michel breathed in my ear. "Your teacher, she dance like an elephant."

It was a compliment in a way. At least he didn't think *I* danced like an elephant. But I didn't have long to enjoy this thought.

"Excuse me," someone hissed, and Julie practically ripped Michel away from me. Behind her, Sean Miles stood alone – Julie had abandoned him in the middle of the dance floor.

"What did I do?" he asked me, bewildered. "I'm like asking her name in French, and suddenly she's off. Did I insult her by accident?"

"It wasn't you," I said. "She didn't like me dancing with her boyfriend."

"Oh, so she's the jealous type? Maybe she's got cause. I saw that guy outside earlier, snogging Olivia Higgs. He must be a fast worker." Sean looked enviously after Michel. "How does he do it?"

Fortunately that was the last of the country dances. A DJ from Year 12 was setting up his decks. This should be good – I couldn't wait to see Mrs Cole disco-dancing.

In the interval I went to the loo. When I came out, Julie was standing outside with two of her friends. I really didn't like the look on her face.

She said something in French. I only caught one word of it, which was *grosse* – meaning fat. Then she turned towards me.

"Don't talk to my boyfriend. Leave him. He does not like you."

"Look," I said, "you've got it wrong. I'm not after your boyfriend. I just happened to dance with him, that's all."

"Don't lie! I see how you smile at him! You will not have him, you fat pig! Fat ugly pig – I hate you!"

Chapter Four

The French exchange part 2

There's something about hatred — it sparks off more hatred in return. Forgetting all my Christian ideals, I wanted to hurt Julie as she was hurting me.

"I wouldn't want a boyfriend like Michel," I said. "He's cheating on you. He was outside, snogging Olivia Higgs."

Julie looked blank. Obviously "snogging" was not on her English vocabulary list.

"Michel was kissing Olivia," I said as slowly as I could, adding untruthfully, "She is much more beautiful than you."

"*Ce n'est pas vrai!* Michel loves me!"

"Oh, does he? Do you know where he is at this moment?"

A look of doubt crept onto her face.

"Try the car park," I said. "I bet he's not alone."

Julie snarled something to her friends. All three of them hurried out. I went in search of Ellie and told her what had happened.

"The worst thing is, I've got to take her home tonight and be polite to her… I really don't think I can do it."

"Hey, I just had a thought," said Ellie. "We could arrange a swap — Julie for Pierre. Then Julie won't be able to stab you in your sleep, and Pierre won't get asthma, and most important, Casper can come out of the kitchen. How about that?"

"Brilliant, except for one small problem. Where's Pierre going to sleep? In the garden shed?"

"Why can't you put him in Josh's room? Josh could go in with your mum and dad. Oh come on, Phoebe. At least we could ask them what they think."

And so, after a few discussions and phone calls, it was arranged. The swap took place that same evening.

After the dance, Julie was in a terrible mood. She'd had a huge row with Michel and finished with him. (It was the highlight of the evening – much more entertaining than the Morris Men.) Michel didn't seem too heartbroken; Venice looked ecstatic.

We went home, where Julie packed up her few possessions and we said a chilly goodbye. Dad took her round to Ellie's house, bringing Pierre back with him. It was French exchange part two.

Josh and Georgie, half asleep, had been hurriedly removed from Josh's room, and Mum had remade the bed. It had a Thomas the Tank Engine bedcover, but Pierre didn't care. He sat down on the bed with a contented sigh.

"In Ellie's house," he said, "the cat likes to sleep on the beds, and so the asthma is very bad. Here it will be better, I think. You don't have the animals, Phoebe?"

"Only a guinea pig."

"A... pig? You have a pig?" He looked surprised.

I tried to remember the French word. "*Un cobaye.*" For some reason I didn't feel nervous about trying out my useless French. Not like with Julie.

"Ah, *oui. Un cobaye.*"

"But it never comes indoors. The only animal that has slept on this bed is my brother."

He laughed. Oh, this was ace! We could talk to each other, understand each other. He even laughed at my stupid jokes.

Next morning, Pierre said he had slept well. He didn't sound at all wheezy, and his face had some colour in it. He even had enough energy to play with Josh, who was fascinated with him.

"Car," said Josh, handing Pierre a toy.

"*Un auto,*" said Pierre, handing it back.

"Ta."

"*Merci bien.*"

"Don't confuse Josh. He can't even speak one language yet," I said. "You know, Pierre, I'm really glad you swapped with Julie. *She* never played with Josh. In fact she didn't try to get on with any of us."

"Ah, Julie. She is beautiful, but not very friendly, I think. Not like you, Phoebe."

OK, so I was friendly but not very beautiful. I knew that – he didn't have to spell it out.

It was Saturday. There were no planned activities for the French pupils, so I asked Pierre what he would like to do. He surprised me by saying he would like to go swimming. Unlike most other sports, swimming didn't make him wheezy, and the doctor had told him to swim twice a week.

I used to love swimming. In Year 7 I was good enough to be on the school team. But then people began to notice my weight problem, or rather, I began to notice them noticing it. I got more sensitive to cruel comments, and hated the sight of myself in a swimsuit.

"You like to swim, Phoebe?" Pierre asked.

"I used to," I said cautiously. "I haven't been swimming in ages."

It occurred to me that in a swimming pool, Pierre couldn't wear his glasses, and without them he was very short-sighted. In any case I didn't mind what Pierre thought about me. I didn't fancy him, I wasn't trying to impress him.

So we went swimming and had a great time. I had forgotten how nice it felt, gliding through the water with long, slow strokes, or kicking out, strong and powerful, motoring along.

We raced each other. Although I was out of training, I was faster than Pierre at breast stroke. He beat me swimming freestyle, and in back stroke we were equal.

"You swim very well," said Pierre.

"Don't sound so surprised! It's the only sport I've ever been any good at."

As I showered afterwards, I felt terrific – full of energy. I told myself I ought to swim more often. Perhaps if I came early on a Saturday morning, I wouldn't bump into anyone I knew...

We had lunch in the swimming pool café, then walked back through town. I showed Pierre the sights of Sandersfield, which didn't take long. The parish church (closed on Saturdays), the market, the museum (closed for renovation), the park, and Hill House, scene of a famous murder (not open to the public).

The murder, even though it took place 50 years ago, was the thing that interested Pierre. The victim was a middle-aged businessman, poisoned by his wife, or so people said. The wife had disappeared along with a large amount of money; she was never caught.

Everyone in Sandersfield knew the story, because of their daughter. It was quite a sad story really. The girl had been about 18 when her father was murdered and her mother disappeared. She refused to believe her mother was guilty. She went on living in Hill House, waiting for her mother's return, for 50 years.

"She was mad, really," I explained. "She used to walk round the town, talking to herself. People say she kept the inside of the house exactly like it was when her parents were alive."

"What happened to her?" asked Pierre.

"She died a couple of years ago."

"So the house is not occupied?"

We peered through the overgrown hedge. Hill House was a good-sized building, set well back from the road. It was easy to see that it was empty, for the lower windows were boarded up. Weeds were growing through the gravel driveway. Even in broad daylight, the place looked quite sinister.

Miss Myers, the mad old lady, had never made a will. Her distant relatives were arguing over who should inherit her house and her money. Until the law courts sorted it out, the house belonged to nobody.

"I would like to see this place, the inside," said Pierre.

"You can't. It's all locked up."

There was a thick chain and padlock on the iron gates to the driveway. Even if you could climb over, the front door of the house was boarded up.

"There is an entrance at the back?" said Pierre hopefully.

"I don't think so. The canal runs along the back of the house. You can walk along the towpath, but I don't think there's a gate or anything." He looked so disappointed that I said, "We can go home that way, if you like. Why are you so interested?"

Because he was a boy. Boys, for some reason, are into horror films and scary experiences. Boys do dangerous things for the thrill of it when life gets too boring. Boys end up in Casualty with broken bones. Most girls have got more sense.

We walked along to the canal, up the steps and back along the towpath. The canal bank was well above ground level, so that we looked down into the back gardens of houses. Then came a thick, impenetrable hedge which looked as if no one had trimmed it for years. It stood well above my head.

"I'm pretty sure we're at the back of Hill House," I said. "But see – no gate."

Pierre craned his neck, rather pointlessly. (If I couldn't see over the hedge, he had even less chance.) After a while he seemed to accept the fact that he wasn't going to see the murder scene.

Just then a woman came past, walking a terrier. The dog picked up an interesting scent and followed it towards the hedge. A second later, it had vanished.

"Minty. Minty! Come out of there!" the woman called, pulling in the extending lead. Minty reappeared, looking sheepish (if a terrier can look sheepish). Pierre went to look at the spot where the dog had done its disappearing trick.

"Look, Phoebe!" he called, excited.

Down at ground level there was a small gap in the hedge, and a worn patch like a path leading through it. Pierre lay down, wriggled along on his stomach, and disappeared through the hedge.

"Pierre! Come back!" I shouted.

But Pierre was not a dog on a lead. He didn't come back.

Oh, help. Now what was I supposed to do?

Chapter Five

Chicken

Very reluctantly, I got down on my hands and knees to look through the gap. Beyond lay a small wood or orchard; Pierre was picking his way between the trees.

"Wait for me!" I called. "Don't go in there alone!"

He waited as I struggled through the hole. There was a bad moment when a branch caught my belt, and I thought I was stuck. Then the branch snapped, and I forced my way through.

Looking around, I could see that this must have been a garden long ago. A wire fence, badly broken down, surrounded a tennis court where the grass grew knee-high. There were old, gnarled apple trees, with fallen apples mouldering in the weeds below. There was a rotting summer house which looked ready to collapse.

But Pierre didn't stop to admire this secret garden – he was heading for the house. I hurried after him.

The back of the house looked even worse than the front – broken guttering, peeling plaster, and a fallen chimney pot which had shattered on the path. I was relieved to see that all the ground floor windows were boarded up. I really did not want Pierre to get inside. It would be dark in there, mouldy-smelling, full of cobwebs… yeucch.

Pierre found a door which wasn't boarded up, but it only led to a tool shed. Another door opened on a wash house with a sink, a fireplace and a rusty mangle.

"Look," he said. "Someone sleeps here."

I ventured just inside the door. He showed me a pile

of old sacks in the corner, with a grubby sleeping bag laid out on top. In the fireplace was a heap of fluffy grey ash. And a neat row of apples (probably out of the garden) lay along the window sill.

"Who can this be?" he asked.

"Some old dosser."

"Dosser. Dosser." When Pierre came across a new word, he would repeat it to himself, learning it.

"A homeless person, I mean, sleeping rough," I explained.

I didn't like the feeling that we had invaded somebody's personal space. I went out, and after a moment Pierre followed me. He looked longingly up at the house, which hung over us like a dark cliff. The garden was very quiet, apart from the whisper of wind through the ivy leaves.

Suddenly Pierre clutched my arm.

"Up there!" He pointed to an upstairs window. "Something moved!"

My heart thudded. Although I don't believe in ghosts – not in daylight anyway – I thought of old Miss Myers, who had died in that house, and her father who was murdered there.

"I c-can't see anything," I said, hearing my voice shake.

Shading my eyes, I looked up at the dark window with its broken pane of glass. No, he must have imagined it...

Then I saw it... a brief flicker of light in the darkness, a white shape moving. It vanished almost before I'd seen it.

"You see it too?" Pierre whispered.

"Yes. I don't like this, Pierre. I'm scared."

He was scared too, I could tell. But he picked up a stone, and with a wild yell sent it crashing through the unbroken side of the window. A second later, a startled bird flew out and swooped into the trees.

"Only a bird, that is all," said Pierre, looking rather let down. Then he must have realised how pale I was. "Sorry, Phoebe, I have made you frightened. Are you OK?"

"I'm all right," I said crossly. "But can we go now?"

Apart from that little episode, I quite enjoyed the French exchange. Pierre got on really well with my family, even Georgie. (I think Georgie would have been pleased to swap him for her current boyfriend, given half a chance.)

I liked him too – as a friend. All my friends up to now had been female. I never felt comfortable and relaxed around boys; I was too worried about looking good, saying the right thing.

But with Pierre I was quite at ease. Was it because I didn't fancy him and he didn't fancy me? Or because we had both been through some hard times? We knew what it was like to feel left out, to be the last one picked when teams were chosen. Pierre felt like an outsider because of his asthma; I felt the same because of my weight.

"Some people grow out of asthma as they get older," I said. "My cousin did."

"And some are not fat when they grow more tall," said Pierre. "You are still growing, Phoebe?"

"Yes." I had realised, a few weeks before, that I was slightly taller than Mum. This had come as a bit of a shock to both of us. (Unfortunately I was more than slightly heavier than Mum, who had been dieting for ages.)

"If you grow tall like Ellie, you will look slim," said Pierre.

"But I don't want to be as tall as that. No thank you."

"Why not? I would like very much to be so tall."
"Yes, but you're a boy."

Why I would rather not be six foot two:

1 There aren't too many Year 10 boys as tall as that.
2 I'd rather look at people's faces than their dandruff.
3 It would be hard to buy trousers long enough and shoes big enough.
4 Not to mention tights.
5 I don't want to be a model or a basketball player.
6 I like to lie stretched out in bed without my feet sticking out the end.
7 It's just not normal for girls to be so tall. And normal is good, right? Everyone wants to be normal.

As the week went on, Venice got more and more depressed. She really liked Michel, and he was interested in her, or so she thought. But then she found out that he had got back together with Julie.

"I hate him," Venice muttered.

"Don't waste your time on him," I said. "He's not worth it. He's a love rat."

"But he's *so* nice."

"Wrong. He may be nice-looking, but he's not nice. Pierre is ten times nicer than he is."

"Oooh!" said Ellie. "Has Phoebe found the man of her dreams?"

"No way," I protested. "We're just good friends."

"Yeah, yeah."

The man of my dreams, I decided, would have Michel's looks and Pierre's friendly, easy-going nature. But could this person exist? And if he did, would he ever notice me?

On the last-but-one day of the exchange, we all went to Langley Park, a stately home and theme park. By now the French and English pupils had got to know each other quite well. On the guided tour of the mansion, the two nationalities were all mixed together. Mrs Cole was delighted.

After the educational (ie boring) bit we went to the theme park. Ellie, Venice and I went around with Julie, Michel and Pierre. (Julie and Michel looked as if they would rather have been alone, but we'd been told to stay in groups of four or more.)

We went on a couple of rides, then had lunch at the burger bar. Michel and Julie exchanged lingering glances throughout the meal. Then they began feeding each other tenderly with fries. Venice looked rather sick.

"Anyone want this?" she said, pushing her food away. "I'm not hungry."

Well, I hate to see good food going to waste... Anyway, think of all the calories we would use up, walking round, queuing and screaming our heads off.

In the centre of the park stood the scariest ride – the Suicide Bomber. Two rows of people were lifted into the air, spun around at high speed and flipped almost upside down. Just looking at it made my stomach feel uneasy.

Michel strode confidently towards it. Julie looked less keen, which made Venice say, "Come on. Let's give it a go."

Ellie, who hates heights, muttered, "Er... I don't think I..."

Just then we were spotted by Sean, Joe and Ryan, who were waiting in the queue. "Don't tell me Phoebe's going on this," shouted Joe. "Isn't there a weight limit?"

"She won't do it. She'll chicken out," said Ryan, and they all started making chicken noises.

This left me with absolutely no option. I joined the queue, along with the others. Ellie whispered, "I'm going to keep my eyes closed the whole time."

Only Pierre did not join the line. He said, "It will make me to feel sick. I think I'll wait here and watch you."

Julie said something scornful in French, and Pierre flushed slightly. But he didn't change his mind. He sat down on a bench as the queue shuffled slowly forwards.

I rather wished the ride would break down before we reached it (preferably while Sean, Joe and Ryan were upside down in mid-air). But eventually it was our turn. With a feeling of doom, I sat down. The safety harness squeezed me tightly around my waist, and I began to regret that last burger I'd eaten. What if the harness could not hold me? SCHOOLGIRL DIES IN SHOCK DEATH RIDE PLUNGE...

Safe on his bench, Pierre gave me a cheerful wave. I could have been there with him – if only I'd had enough courage to look like a coward.

The machine shuddered into motion. To begin with it wasn't too bad – no worse than the Dracula Ride. But then it speeded up and started moving in three directions at once, whirling and tossing us, flipping us like pancakes.

Make it stop. Please, please make it stop, before all my insides end up on the outside...

At last the ride slowed down, brought us horizontal again and came to a stop. My stomach was heaving; I could hardly walk straight. I made it as far as a clump of bushes, where I was violently sick.

"Phoebe? Are you OK?" Ellie asked cautiously from a safe distance.

"No," I groaned, trying to keep out of sight. Too late – Sean and Joe saw me and started laughing their heads off. I've never felt such an idiot in my entire life.

Chapter Six

Unlucky in love

It took me ages to feel normal again. While Julie, Michel and Venice went on all the scary rides, Ellie, Pierre and I tried out the slow, gentle ones designed for grannies and 5-year-olds.

"You don't need to stick with me," I protested. "You're missing all the best rides."

"That's the whole idea," said Ellie. "You're my excuse for staying at ground level."

Pierre asked her, "Why did you go on the big ride, if you don't like it?"

"Oh, you know… I didn't want to be left out if everyone else was going on it."

Pierre was too honest sometimes – he didn't know the meaning of the word "tactful". "And you, Phoebe? You made yourself sick, only because you don't want to be left out?"

"OK. OK. I know it was stupid."

Just then Venice arrived, all on her own. She said angrily, "Julie told me to go away. She's got a nerve! Michel is my guest, after all."

"You shouldn't have let her see that you fancy him," I said. "She's as jealous as anything – you're lucky she didn't try to poison your Coke. Where are they now?"

"Queuing for the Big Wheel. Oh, I wish Michel wasn't going home tomorrow. I'm going to miss him so much."

I would miss Pierre too, though not with Venice's desperate longing. How could she be so crazy about a rat like Michel? And she had only met him a week ago. Love does strange things to people…

Half an hour later, we noticed a bit of a commotion around the Big Wheel. The people in the queue were being turned away. A large sign read, "This attraction is closed for maintenance". The wheel itself had stopped – but there were people still on board, trapped in fragile-looking cabins swaying slightly in the wind. Right at the top we could just make out Julie and Michel's faces.

"Julie did you a good turn, Venice," I said. "You could have been trapped up there, too."

Venice said recklessly, "I wouldn't have minded. Not if Michel was there."

The wheel was stuck for nearly two hours. We kept an eye on it as we went around the park. When it eventually got moving again, Venice dragged us all back there to make sure her beloved Michel was still in one piece.

Michel and Julie got out of their cabin, arguing like crazy. Two hours of being trapped together, 50 metres in the air, clearly hadn't done much for their relation-ship. They stormed off in opposite directions.

"Michel! Wait!" called Venice, running after him.

"She's making a fool of herself," said Ellie. "Anyone can see he doesn't care about her."

But later, when we all met up at the coach, Venice and Michel were walking hand in hand. Venice had a huge grin all over her face. I couldn't help feeling slightly envious. Even though she would only be with him for a day, Venice had found herself a boyfriend.

Would it ever be my turn?

Three weeks later, I had changed my mind about envying Venice. She had written to Michel several times, with no reply (even when she became desperate enough to try writing in French). Then he wrote telling her he had found someone else – please to stop writing the letters.

She was very upset. One day's happiness, then weeks of heartbreak… it didn't seem worth it.

"He never cared about me," she said. "I loved him so much, but he couldn't care less. He was just using me to get back at Julie."

I thought this was probably true, but I tried to cheer her up. "He must have liked you, even if he didn't love you. I mean, he kissed you, didn't he?"

"I don't want him to *like* me." She scowled into the mirror as if she hated her own face. "Wish I was better-looking. Wish I looked like that cow Julie."

"Even if you were Julie's long-lost identical twin, he still wouldn't love you like you love him. He cheated on Julie at the party, remember? He's not in love with anyone except himself."

"Stop it! You're making him sound horrible. He's not like that… he's really nice…"

Love is blind, they say. And when it wants to, it can be stone deaf as well.

Love – who needs it? Friendship is far less stressful. Talking of which, Pierre had emailed me the day after he got home. He said how much he'd enjoyed staying with us. He was arranging that when I went to Paris next term, I would stay with him rather than with Julie, my original guest. "I hope this will be suitable," he wrote. "I hope Ellie will like to stay with Julie."

Ellie was quite happy with this arrangement; Julie had promised to take her shopping in Paris. I probably wouldn't get to do too much shopping with Pierre, but that was a small price to pay.

As for Venice, she was half dreading, half longing for

the return visit to Michel. I just hoped she had got over him by that time.

I hadn't forgotten my decision to swim more often. Twice I had managed to heave myself out of bed on a Saturday morning and get down to the pool. It was fairly quiet at 9 am. I swam up and down without stopping – ten times on the first day, 14 on the second. If I went on improving at this rate, I would be swimming a mile at a time by Christmas... and I would be bored out of my mind. It was dreary, swimming up and down with no one to talk to.

At 9.30 a swimming club took over the pool, so I had to get out. One of the members stopped me on the way to the changing rooms. It was a Year 8 girl called Verity, who went to my church.

"Phoebe! Why don't you join our club? We need people your age. You're a good swimmer – I was watching you."

I hesitated. "What sort of things do you do?"

"We train on Saturday mornings. It's only an hour, but it really improves your fitness. And there are galas every few weeks – racing against other clubs. The problem is, we never win because we hardly have anyone to compete in the older age groups."

I saw that the other members were mostly quite young. There was no one from my year – which was fine with me. Verity explained that the club had only been going for a few months. "But it's really good, and the coach is brilliant. Come and meet her."

Impressed by Verity's keenness, I did go and talk to the coach. She encouraged me to stay for the practice session and see how I liked it. Apart from the shock of discovering that some of the 11-year-olds could swim faster than me, I enjoyed myself.

"Mum, I want to join a swimming club," I said when I got home.

Mum looked pleased. "What a good idea. Which club is it?"

"I don't know the name. Verity Brown goes to it."

"Verity Brown? But she's as thin as a rake. They certainly shouldn't have her as a member. Where does this club meet?"

"In the swimming pool, of course." (This is it — Mum's finally cracking up, I thought.) "Where else would they swim? In the canal?"

"Oh, a *swimming* club." The light dawned. "I thought you said a slimming club."

No way. I had once tried the slimming club that Mum went to, but there was no one there below the age of 30. They all sat around drinking skimmed-milk coffee, discussing recipes and stretch marks and awful teenage kids.

Maybe if there was a slimming club designed for teenagers, I would give it a try. We could drink Diet Coke and discuss clothes, boys and awful parents. But no such club existed.

I would just have to hope that the regular swimming would do me some good. Even fat people can get fit… some day I'd be able to take on the 11-year-olds and beat them.

Chapter Seven

Crime wave

There's a Christian Union at my school. I quite often go to it; sometimes Ellie and Venice come too. It meets on Monday lunchtimes in the RE department, which puts some people off. But it's not at all like RE. Mr Price, the Drama teacher, is in charge, so we don't just sit around talking.

This week the subject was peer pressure. We had to get into groups and make up a short sketch to show what this meant.

Our group decided to show someone being persuaded to start smoking because all his friends were doing it. I thought this was rather boring and unimaginative, but the others disagreed, so I shut up and joined in. (In other words I gave in to peer pressure.)

More interesting was the second group's idea. A group of Year 12 girls were discussing their love lives. Three of them said they had slept with their boyfriends, so the fourth one decided she would do the same. If everyone did it, why shouldn't she? But actually two of the three had been lying. They had never slept with anyone, but they didn't want to admit it – so uncool, if everyone else was doing it.

The final sketch showed a boy at different stages of his life, always wanting things he didn't have. "But Dad, everyone's got this! No one will want to know me if I don't have an authentic football strip... a new games console... a BMX... a decent sound system... an all-night party with loads of drinks..." He ended up with a drug habit and a criminal record, because all his friends had one.

Afterwards, Mr Price asked if peer pressure had ever made anyone do something they were ashamed of. Almost every hand in the room went up. Shoplifting... picking on other kids... vandalism... drinking too much... Internet porn... all because "everyone else was doing it and I didn't want to be the odd one out".

I thought about the time when, egged on by two so-called friends, I nicked some apples from outside a shop. I was around 11 – well old enough to know better, petrified with fear and guilt, but I still did it. And I don't even like apples.

The bell went while we were in the middle of the discussion. Venice, Ellie and I continued it on the way to Registration. Ellie was quite shocked at some of the things people had done.

"I bet there were even worse things that people didn't own up to," I said.

"But these are members of the Christian Union! They shouldn't be doing things like that." Although Ellie often attended the CU, she didn't really count herself as a member – more an interested bystander.

I said, "Just because people are Christians, it doesn't mean they suddenly become perfect."

"But Christians are supposed to be better than other people," said Venice. "Giving to charity and going to church and being kind to people you hate – that's what it's all about. Isn't it?"

"Er... not really." I felt she had got hold of the wrong end of the stick. "What I mean is, that's part of it. But doing all those things doesn't make you a Christian."

"What *does* make you a Christian, then?" Venice asked.

How could you explain it in 30 seconds? Knowing God, understanding his love, being forgiven for all the wrong things you've done... becoming the person he wants you to be...

But we had reached the classroom. The discussion had to stop – none of us wanted people to overhear us. They might laugh. Peer pressure in action yet again...

After school, Mum asked Georgie to nip down to the corner shop for some milk.

"Can't Phoebe go? I went last time," Georgie moaned.

I said smugly, "I'm doing my homework."

Now that I was in Year 10, words like "homework" and "GCSE coursework" acted on Mum like a magic spell. "Homework is more important," she said firmly. "You go, please, Georgie. Take the money out of my purse."

"I can't find your purse," Georgie complained. "It's not in your bag."

"Yes it is. Have a proper look."

Georgie's idea of a proper look meant tipping the bag upside down on the sofa. She found a lot of things, but no purse.

Useful objects found in handbag of 38-year-old mother of three:

1 Wallet holding credit card, library card and gym membership (expired).
2 Comb, lipstick and nail file.
3 Small child's sock (one only).
4 Unpaid phone bill.
5 Crumpled map of London Zoo. (You never know

when you might need to find the Penguin Pool in a hurry.)

6 Broken necklace.

7 Emergency nappy for Josh.

8 Squashed packet of Sun Maid raisins.

9 15 tissues, some of them clean.

10 Key ring with combined Swiss army knife/torch/compass (essential when marooned in the trackless wastes of the M25).

"It really isn't there," Georgie said. Mum came to see for herself.

"Well, that's very odd. I know I had it this morning, because I got the child benefit at the post office. And I didn't lose it on the way home. I remember taking some money out…"

Her voice trailed off. She must have put the money in her secret hiding place which she thinks we don't know about (silver teapot, top shelf, kitchen cupboard). She rushed away to check it was still there, and came back looking relieved.

"It's OK, we haven't been burgled," she said. "But I can't think where that purse has got to. There must be £30 or £40 in it."

"Josh might have hidden it somewhere," I suggested.

We all looked at Josh, who was lining up a long row of cars outside his toy garage. He had never shown much interest in handbags, purses or money, because none of them had wheels on.

"I don't think Josh could have reached your bag," said Georgie. "It was up on the computer desk."

We looked all around the house without finding the purse. As I checked Mum's coat pockets, the local paper thudded onto the doormat. I glanced at the front page.

MYSTERY THEFTS
Crime wave hits Sandersfield

Sandersfield police report a sudden rise in opportunist thefts from homes. Most occurred during daylight hours, when windows or doors were left unlocked. The largest loss was £250 in cash, stolen from pensioner Frank O'Malley (78).

"I think the thief must have got in while I was in the house. I don't go out much, and if I do, I'm always careful to lock up. But when I'm at home or out in the garden, I used to leave my door unlocked. Never again!"

"Mum!" I yelled. "Come and see this!"

According to the paper, there had been five other robberies in Sandersfield that week, all following a similar pattern – no sign of a break-in, and nothing stolen except cash. In several cases there were people at home at the time of the theft, but no one had seen or heard anything.

Our front door had a Yale lock which clicked into place automatically when the door was shut. But the kitchen door, opening on to the path at the side of the house, was often unlocked when Mum was around.

"Were you indoors all the time?" I asked her.

"Yes, except for when I popped out to hang up some washing. I was only out there for five minutes."

"And you didn't lock the back door?"

"No, I never do. Josh was indoors in his playpen. It always seems risky locking the door, just in case I lock myself out, or the house catches fire or something." Did I mention that my mum is a bit of a worrier?

"Oh dear," she said, turning suddenly quite pale. "Someone was here, in our living room, when Josh was all by himself. They could easily have run off with him!" She scooped him up and cuddled him tightly. He began to howl in protest at being separated from his cars.

"Why would anyone want to steal Josh?" I asked.

Georgie's eyes widened. "If Josh was in here, he must have actually seen the thief. Josh! What did he look like?"

But of course Josh was far too young to be any help.

"Car," he said, struggling in Mum's arms. She put him down reluctantly and reached for the phone.

"I'm going to call the police," she said.

Chapter Eight

Dog watch

It was rather disappointing. I expected that a fingerprint expert would check the entire house, like on TV, and then take all our fingerprints to compare them with what he found. But no one bothered.

Mum said, "Apparently they've already found some clear fingerprints at the scene of earlier thefts. Quite small ones – probably a young teenager."

"So why don't they arrest him?" demanded Georgie.

"They may have no idea who it is," said Dad. "If the thief has never been caught, his fingerprints won't be on the police computer."

Mum said, "They asked me if I'd noticed anyone following me on the way back from the post office. I said no. Josh was playing up, trying to climb out of the buggy. I wouldn't have noticed if a brass band had been following me."

"So they think the thief follows people home?" I asked.

"It's a possibility, they said. Three of the other victims were old people who were robbed on pension day."

What a rotten thing to do… hang around at a post office until some poor old pensioner hobbled out, follow him home and take all his money. And Mum – had he followed Mum, too? Waited until he saw her go outside with a load of washing? Slid indoors, found her purse, and given Josh a cheeky grin on the way out? Just the thought of it made me angry.

"Oh well, it's only money," said Mum. "We can

probably claim it on the house insurance. But I'll definitely keep that door locked in future."

"Aren't the police going to *do* anything?" asked Georgie. "This thief is just wandering into people's houses, and no one's able to stop him?"

"I don't know what the police can do, unless they catch him in the act," said Dad. He was being irritatingly calm about the whole thing.

Mum said, "They did knock on a few doors along the street, asking if anyone noticed anything suspicious. But no luck."

"What makes them so sure it's a teenager?" I wondered. "Teenagers always get the blame for everything. It could be an adult with small fingers. Or a trained monkey... or a little old lady."

Dad said, "If it was an adult, you'd expect him to steal other things besides money — credit cards and cheque books and so on."

Even though we hadn't lost much, the theft made us all feel uneasy. Dad looked at adverts for home security systems, then decided they were too expensive — it was cheaper being burgled. Mum became obsessive about locking doors and windows. Georgie started hiding her possessions in weird places, such as under the bedroom rug – then she got upset when I trod on her Walkman.

It must be even more nerve-wracking for elderly people, especially if they lived alone. "A lot of old people don't have decent insurance, either," said Mum. "That man in the paper may never get his £250 back."

I was annoyed that the police seemed to treat our case so lightly. OK, so it was only £30, and other people had lost much more. But it was still a crime – and if the thief wasn't caught, he would carry on stealing.

Just in case the police had missed anything, I went

round various neighbours, asking about the day of the robbery. The problem is, King's Avenue is pretty quiet during the day because most people are at work or at school. I thought my best bet would be Mrs Gillespie, who lives opposite us. She's a nosy old bat who spends her life peeping out from behind her lace curtains. If anyone had seen the thief, it would be her.

"Monday? No, dear, I went shopping that morning, and I bumped into a friend, so we went and had a cup of tea..." I heard all about her friend, the friend's bad leg, the friend's husband's operation... At last she got back to the subject.

"If you ask me, your thief must have been one of those gypsies, or travelling people, or whatever they call themselves nowadays. There's a whole encampment of them up on the bypass, littering the place and letting their dirty kids play in the mud like animals. Two of them came round last week, asking if I wanted any work done, but I said no thank *you!* Spying out the land, that's what they were doing."

When I told Dad what she had suggested, he said I shouldn't jump to conclusions.

"Travellers get the blame for everything from litter to stolen cars. You think it's unfair that teenagers get blamed all the time – it's far worse for the travelling people."

That's the trouble with Dad – he always has to be fair. (He's deputy head of a school which has a lot of problem pupils. The effort of being fair to everyone – pupils, teachers, parents, governors, caretaker, school cat – nearly kills him sometimes.)

I said, "So it's pure coincidence that all these thefts suddenly start when the travellers are in the area?"

"Who knows?" said Dad. "But unless you've got some

evidence, you shouldn't point the finger at anyone."

Evidence… I decided to look for some.

Ellie has a part-time job after school, walking dogs for people who are on holiday, ill, or just plain lazy. Sometimes I help her. The money isn't great, but at least it's good exercise.

For several days I went walking with Bart, a plump, good-natured Labrador. Each day we spent at least half an hour in the park opposite the post office. (If you need an excuse for hanging around someplace, especially around trees and lamp-posts, then all you need is a dog.) I kept one eye on the door of the post office, hoping for someone to come out, absent-mindedly pocketing a pension book or a fat wallet… and for someone else to start following them.

That sunny autumn afternoon, there were quite a few people just waiting around. A gang of Year 9 boys admiring each other's bikes… a group of younger girls admiring the boys… two old men on a bench… a woman at the bus stop…

"Those fingerprints," I said, "could have come from a woman, not a teenager. Some women have quite small hands."

"If you say so." Ellie was getting bored with my surveillance operation, and so was the dog she was exercising. "I'm going to take Zeke down to the river. Are you coming? The post office will be closing pretty soon, anyway."

"No, I'll hang on here, I think."

Just before 5 pm, a couple came out of the post office. They had a tartan shopping trolley and matching His'n'Hers tweed hats – yes, they were definitely pensioners. Would any of the fish take the bait?

The only person who moved was the woman at the

bus stop. She glanced at her watch, frowned with annoyance, and set out walking. What a surprise – she took the same road as the elderly couple.

I had let Bart off his lead, which was a mistake. Normally he was quite easy to catch, but today he wanted to play. I had to chase him halfway around the park. At last I managed to corner him and snap the lead on to his collar. My suspect was still in view, a long way down Gilbert Street.

"Come on, Bart. Hurry!"

All of a sudden, with a snarling growl, a small dog appeared out of the bushes and went for Bart. It had a bandaged leg and was about half the size of Bart, but there was no contest. Poor Bart tried to hide behind my legs while the small terror snapped and yelped around us. The owner, a girl about Georgie's age, came running up.

"Matt! Matt! Come here!" she cried, but Matt was all fired up and wouldn't listen. She finally collared him and tugged him away, still growling. "Sorry," she gasped. "Last time he tried that, he got bitten. I thought it might teach him some sense."

"OK, no harm done," I said. Over-optimistically. For the old couple and the woman were nowhere in sight.

They must have turned off Gilbert Street into one of the many side streets or alleys leading down to the river. Which one? Bart and I raced along, looking down each turning, but they had vanished in the maze of little streets.

Bart, panting, dragged me to a halt. It was no good – I had lost them. Perhaps the woman was quite innocent… perhaps not. Would I know her if I saw her again? She had curly red hair, a thin face and a tattered old denim jacket. That was all I could remember.

I would have to look out for the next issue of the *Sandersfield News*. If any more robberies were reported, I would go to the police and tell them I might have seen the thief in action. Well, not in action exactly, but stalking her prey.

Oh yes? What I had actually seen was a woman walking down the street, that was all. Nothing criminal about that. "Evidence," Dad had said. "Get some evidence before you start pointing the finger."

Bart whined and lay down on the pavement, still panting.

"You're unfit," I told him. "I've got more energy than you have."

Perhaps I really was getting fitter. The swimming and walking must be doing me good – I certainly wouldn't have been able to run like that a few months ago.

The next week I scanned the local paper eagerly. No more thefts were reported, but a small paragraph mentioned that the council had evicted the travellers from the Sandersfield bypass. They had been forced to move on somewhere else. I just hoped the thief had gone with them.

Chapter Nine

Personal best

There was a swimming gala coming up. I persuaded Mum that I really needed a new swimsuit in honour of the occasion. My current one was so ancient, it was practically see-through.

Club members were supposed to wear a standard design in black, supplied by the sports shop in the High Street. Surprise, surprise – they didn't come in a size 20.

"Are you sure you need a 20?" asked the assistant. "I'd have said you were more like an 18."

I tried one on, although I just knew it would be hopelessly tight, emphasising every bulge of fat. I was wrong; it fitted me perfectly. It didn't look too bad, either – but then black is supposed to be slimming. (Did that mean I should eat nothing but black foods, such as caviar and ultra-dark chocolate?)

"It must be a fluke," I muttered to Ellie. "Can you get me another size 18 in a different design?"

She brought me two, and both of them fitted me. Amazing!

"I don't understand," I said. "I haven't been slimming, so how can I get into an 18?"

"You do look a bit thinner, you know," said Ellie. "I thought so the other day when we were getting changed for PE."

"Did I hear you right? Say it again."

"You do look thinner. You do look thinner. Look, if you want me as your personal trainer, I'd better warn you I charge 50 quid an hour."

I bought the black swimsuit and hurried home to weigh myself. It was disappointing to find that my weight hadn't changed since last term.

"But you've grown taller since then," said Mum. "If you're taller but no heavier, you're bound to look slimmer."

"I don't just look thinner – I've gone down a whole size. How did it happen?"

"Perhaps you've got a tapeworm living inside you," said Georgie. "We're doing them in Biology. They crawl about in your guts—"

"Georgie! Save it till after supper," said Mum, dishing out platefuls of wriggling spaghetti. "It must be all the exercise you've been doing, Phoebe. Have your clothes been feeling bigger on you?"

"I haven't noticed. But then most of my things have got elastic waists. I suppose my jeans do feel a bit loose, now you mention it."

Later I tried the swimsuit on again in the privacy of the bathroom. It really did look as if my stomach was less flabby than it used to be, and my thighs were not so huge. Don't get me wrong, I was still fat... I still looked like the "before" photo of a slimming ad. But I had made a small step in the right direction.

Oh, if only I could keep it up! I would swim three times a week, I would walk Bart for miles, I would be glad to grow taller – if only I could be slim. My life would change totally. Boys would fancy me and girls like Julie would be more friendly; I would be pretty and successful and popular and good at Maths...

Yeah. Dream on.

Pauline, the swimming coach, persuaded me to enter for three events at the gala. Three! "Even if you don't get through to the finals, it will be good experience," she said. "Besides, you're the best girl we've got in your age group." She grinned at me. I knew quite well I was the *only* girl in the age group.

"You're a slave-driver," I moaned. "I'm amazed you didn't put me down for all four legs of the relay."

"The thought did cross my mind," said Pauline.

The competition was held at Marling, in the Olympic sized pool. It looked enormous as I swam up and down in the warm up session, but it had the advantage that in each race we would only have to turn once. I still wasn't wonderful on turns.

I knew I had improved a lot during the weeks I'd been training with the club. I could now beat all the little kids, but I had no girls of my own age to compete with. What if I was total rubbish, last in every race?

The warm up ended. I went to sit in the area assigned to our club.

"Hi, Phoebe." It was a Year 11 guy called Sam. He had recently joined the club, or rather been dragged in by his enthusiastic sister. He was a quiet guy, rather lacking in confidence – perhaps because of his spots, which were ferocious. You couldn't tell if he was good-looking or not. When you looked at his face, all you saw were spots before your eyes.

I sat down next to him and we watched the younger members competing. Our 10- and 11-year-olds were doing really well. When the team totals were displayed on the scoreboard, Sandersfield were in second place.

"Girls, 14 to 15, 100 metre breast stroke," came the announcement. "Heat One."

Six of us lined up. I felt my stomach clench with fear. Not last – please don't let me come last…

"Take your marks… go!"

It was a good dive, I just knew it. Amazingly, it put me in the lead, and I managed to stay there for the whole of the first length. But I messed up the turn. The girl on my right began to draw ahead of me.

Don't panic. Pace yourself... keep focused...

Hard as I tried, I could not close the gap. The girl beat me by at least a metre. But I had come second! I was through to the final!

There would be a half-hour wait between the heats and the final. I sat down to watch the next event. I was exhausted but also excited — a weird combination, like cold tea mixed with a shaken can of Coke. I began to feel rather sick.

Oh God, please help me to do well in the final... please...

I suddenly wondered if the other finalists were praying the same prayer. Which one would be heard? Does God have favourites? Or would he arrange for an amazing photo-finish, all six of us first equal?

The thought made me smile. I knew that in the grand design of the universe, the result of the 100 m breast stroke couldn't be all that vital. But this is the wonderful thing: God cares about the things we care about. And he understands how we feel, because Jesus went through it all when he was on earth. He understands anxiety, fear and rejection, pain, loneliness... he lived through it all. Like Pierre, who understood English well because he had lived in England, Jesus understands people because he lived on earth.

So I changed my prayer. You know how I feel, Lord. Please help me to stay calm, to do my best and not be afraid...

After that, I did feel calmer. I woke up to what was happening around me — the cheers as Verity won the 12 to 13 freestyle, the disappointment as Sam just failed to qualify in the back stroke. Then it was my turn again.

I walked to the starting block. Up in the viewing gallery, Dad gave me an encouraging wave. But I could tell by his face that he was as tense as I was.

"Take your marks… go!"

Another good dive, but when I surfaced there were at least two people ahead of me. Don't look at them – concentrate. Remember your training. Long, firm strokes, strong kicks, powerful arms. Keep the rhythm… look out, it's the turn… keep the rhythm, faster now, nearly there…

I touched the rail and looked quickly to both sides. I had come in either third or fourth. My teammates were cheering, and Sam held up three fingers. Third?

"Well done," said Pauline. "That looked to me like a personal best. We'll get the official timing in a minute."

It *was* a personal best, and I did get third place, which meant a medal and a point for our team. I felt a bright glow of achievement. I'd almost stopped caring about the other two races. Even if I came last in both of them, I wouldn't go home empty-handed.

Actually I did come last in the freestyle, and I didn't make the back stroke final. But then some of my opponents had been training for years. I knew I could improve if I put my mind to it.

We cheered Sam as he came second in the 14 to 15 freestyle. More team points… but not enough. Sandersfield had no other swimmers in the 14 plus age group. By the end of the day we had slid down the ranking to fifth.

In the changing room there was a mile-long queue for the showers. I waited in line, leaning against a locker because I was tired all of a sudden. It had been a good day, though – a day to remember.

Just then, among the chattering voices around me, I suddenly heard my own name. It's weird how your ears can home in on that one word, like a mother sheep recognising the bleat of one lamb.

"...Phoebe and Sam," the voice said. "Do you think they're an item?"

"What on earth makes you say that?" It was Verity speaking, somewhere out of sight around the back of the lockers.

"Well, she did sit next to him. I thought they looked... not exactly good together," she giggled, "but sort of right for each other. Fat Phoebe and Spotty Sam – they even sound right, don't they?"

I felt my face turn bright red, as red as Sam's spots.

"Shhh! Don't be so mean," said Verity. "It's not their fault."

"Oh yes it is," said the other voice. I guessed it belonged to Charlotte, a spiteful Year 9 girl who was always stirring up trouble. "You can get medical treatment for spots, and go on a diet if you're fat. Nobody *has* to go around looking like they've escaped from a freak show."

I didn't wait to hear any more. Charlotte mustn't see me – my face would give away the fact that I'd been listening. She would probably be delighted.

Abandoning the shower queue, I found an empty cubicle and locked the door. I wished I could wash the smell of chlorine off my skin... and wash her words out of my memory.

Chapter Ten

Dog fight

Whenever I got depressed, I used to comfort myself by eating things... nice healthy things like biscuits, crisps and cakes. (Fruit and green vegetables may contain lots of vitamins, but for some reason their comfort content is zero.) Mum used to say she could judge my moods by the number of biscuits left in the tin.

I had resolved to break this bad habit. Instead of eating, I tried to find other ways of cheering myself up... call a friend, go for a walk, rent a video, spend some money. But when I got home from the gala, I forgot all that and headed straight for the kitchen cupboard. I really wanted an orange Club biscuit, or three.

Reasons for breaking my resolution:

1 I was sure to have burnt off hundreds of calories in the last few hours.
2 I had something to celebrate.
3 I had something to feel depressed about.
4 I was suffering from withdrawal symptoms – it was weeks since my last orange Club biscuit fix.
5 Just one wouldn't hurt much, would it?
6 I had got a bit thinner, but hardly anyone had noticed, so what was the point?

Shock! Horror! There were no chocolate biscuits in the tin... not a single one. A few nasty Nice biscuits lay broken at the bottom.

"We decided to stop buying them, remember?" said Mum. "Have some fruit instead. There are some lovely ripe plums in the fruit bowl."

"I hate plums," I muttered, feeling a major Bad Mood looming over me like a huge, dark, alien spaceship. I mooched into the living room and kicked Georgie off the computer so I could check my emails. Oh good – there was one from Pierre.

> Dear Phoebe,
> M. Duval has told us we must learn English phrases to make our conversation better. He has given us a list as long as an arm. So I will use you as a guinea pig.
> Here, it is raining cats and dogs. It never rains but it pours. It's hot enough to fry an egg. What a load of cod wallops. Truth to tell, the weather is quite pleasant. I have taken the mickey, I have pulled the wool over your eyes.
> Today, my brother Andre drove me up the wall. He made my blood boil. We fought like cat and dog. For heaven's sake, my father said, you should see eye to eye. My brother threw in the towel. His bark is worse than his bite. So, all's well that ends well. Now we get on like houses on fire.
> This is as easy as a pie. It's child's play and a piece of cake. So now, do I speak English like a native? A penny for your thoughts, Phoebe.
> With kindest regards,
> Pierre.

This made me laugh. I decided I would write a suitable reply using our list of French phrases. But first I sent him a long email about the swimming gala. I hadn't felt like telling anyone else about Charlotte's nasty comments, yet somehow it was easy to write to Pierre about them.

It felt good to get it off my chest.

Pierre replied almost at once.

```
Dear Phoebe,
You must not listen to this girl.
You are not a freak. I suppose this
Charlotte is very ugly, so she
insults the other people to make her
feel better. Don't let her hurt you.
It's better to be beautiful on the
inside than on the outside.
```

That was nice of him – except he was missing the point. You can be as beautiful as you like on the inside, but if people don't like the outside of you, they're never going to find out what a Really Nice Person you are inside.

He could be right about Charlotte, though. Although she wasn't exactly ugly, she had no figure at all – her chest was flatter than a floorboard. This made her look much younger than her friends, especially when they were all wearing swimsuits. Maybe she had a complex about it.

Ha! Charlotte was a freak, too! All kinds of nasty remarks came to mind... I thought of how she would feel if I "accidentally" let her hear them.

After enjoying this plan for a while, I decided regretfully that I couldn't really put it into action. It would be unkind, unloving and unChristian. No – a far better revenge would be to go on getting slimmer and fitter. As Charlotte had said, I didn't *have* to look like a freak.

With any luck I would end up looking normal, while Charlotte was still a size 32AAA. And there would be nothing she could do about it, apart from padding herself out with wads of tissues. (Not a good idea while swimming.)

Fired with enthusiasm, I decided to increase my exercise rate. More dog walking, more swimming...

walk instead of getting the bus... stop hiding in the toilets during Games lessons. Forget Fat Phoebe – it would be Fit Phoebe from now on.

Venice seemed to have got over Michel. She was now keen on somebody else, or rather two people – Dan and Harry Low. They were identical twins.

"Which of them do you like best?" I asked her.

"I don't mind. I'd go out with either of them. You know me – I'm not fussy."

"Yes, but *they* might be."

Venice tried to thump me. "Stop it, or I'll set the dog on you," I warned her.

Ellie had a netball match that Saturday, so Venice and I were walking a dog for her – Rolf, a German shepherd. Venice wanted to take him along the canal towpath. Apparently Harry and Dan often went fishing there.

But there was no sign of them today. We passed a few fishermen; Rolf kept wanting to sniff at the heaving mass of maggots in their bait boxes. He was quite a strong dog, with a mind of his own, so I was glad that Venice was there to help me haul him away.

We came to the hedge which hid the garden of Hill House. I told Venice about Pierre's interest in the place, and about the bird that had scared me half to death. Venice was intrigued.

"Maybe there is an actual ghost there," she said. "How did you get in?"

Pointing out the hole in the hedge, I felt a sudden sharp tug on the lead. I tried to tighten my grip – but too late. Rolf had dived through the gap, with the lead trailing behind him.

Frantically I got down and wriggled through the hole, yelling Rolf's name. Venice followed. We raced through the orchard, kicking up a dust storm of dry leaves. But I couldn't see him.

Then I heard a menacing growl. Behind the summer house, I found him face to face with another, much smaller dog. Both of them were bristling with anger, growling deep in their throats.

"Rolf! Bad dog! Come here."

He didn't take a blind bit of notice. Suddenly the small dog leapt at him, and war broke out. Snapping, growling, yelping with pain and fury, the two dogs spun around like a wild tornado. I didn't know how to stop them without getting bitten.

"Matt! Matt! Stop it!" The other dog's owner had appeared. A young girl – I vaguely recognised her from the previous dog encounter in the park.

Much braver than me, or else more desperate to save her dog, she tried to grab hold of him. The snarling grew louder, and the girl leapt back with a cry of anguish, holding her arm. I reached for the loose end of Rolf's lead as it whipped past me, but I missed it. More yelps of pain – the small dog was getting the worst of it, but he wouldn't give up. There was blood on his coat.

Oh, God! Please help! I don't know what to do!

"Water," said Venice. "We should throw water over them."

I looked around frantically. There was an old water butt beside the summer house. Yes – it had a few inches of slimy green water in the bottom of it. Venice and I lifted it between us, hoping it wouldn't fall apart in our hands, and turned it upside down over the dogs.

You could see the shock on their faces; there was a moment's pause in the fight. Venice and I both leapt for Rolf's lead, and the other girl grabbed her dog. We hauled the two dogs away from each other. Rolf had a torn ear and a wounded paw, but his thick fur had protected him. The small dog was bleeding in about six different places.

"We ought to get them to a vet," I said.

The other girl glared at me. She looked as if she hated me like her dog hated Rolf. "Can't you keep your dog under control?" she almost spat at me.

"He's not mine. Anyway, you can talk – your dog started it."

"That's different. Matt was just protecting his—" She stopped suddenly. "Get out! Go away and leave us alone!"

"Don't worry," said Venice. "We're going."

Chapter Eleven

The St Margaret's type

Rolf's ear looked as if it would need stitches. I thought his owner would be furious, but he was actually quite understanding. He said, "I know Rolf can be a bit aggressive. Well done for managing to stop the fight."

"Venice's idea," I said, and Venice looked modest. "But it was partly my fault for letting go of the lead. Do you want me to pay the vet's bill?"

He laughed, then winced. (He had just had his appendix out, which was the reason he needed a dog walker.) "You wouldn't say that if you knew what vets charge. No, don't worry – our pet insurance will cover it. Come on then, Rolf boy, let's take you down to see the vet, eh?"

Rolf whined piteously. But I didn't feel too sorry for him. If he hadn't run off, he wouldn't have got himself hurt in the first place.

I was more worried about the little dog, badly wounded perhaps, and the girl with the bitten arm.

"Who was that girl?" Venice asked, as we walked back to my house. "Does she go to our school?"

"I don't know. I've definitely seen her before, but not in school – in the park. My sister might know her, though. She looked about Georgie's age, 11 or 12."

We tried to describe the girl to Georgie. She had long, rather tangled, reddish-brown hair. Her face was totally covered in freckles. She was stick-thin, her clothes were scruffy, and her accent didn't sound local. We had only heard her say a few words; Venice thought she had a West Country accent, I believed she might be Irish.

"Doesn't sound like anyone at our school," said Georgie. "Maybe she goes to St Margaret's."

"No, she didn't look the St Margaret's type," I said. (It was a private school – you had to be rich to go there. Somehow, neither the girl nor her dog looked as if they had an expensive pedigree.)

"Perhaps she doesn't go to school at all," said Venice. "She might be one of the travelling people."

"But they got moved on."

"They didn't move very far. They're in a field outside Matton."

Matton, where Venice lived, was three miles away. If the girl was living there, what was she doing in Sandersfield, lurking around Hill House? It didn't make sense.

And I thought of something odd that the girl had said. "Matt was just protecting his—" and then she'd stopped, as if afraid of giving away a secret.

His home? His territory? Suddenly I remembered the old wash house which Pierre had explored, with its pile of sacks laid out like bedding. Could the girl and the dog be living there? Perhaps they were runaways, living rough in the outhouses of the empty building.

When I told Venice of my suspicions, she looked doubtful. "That was weeks ago," she reminded me. "The French exchange was in September – we're halfway through November now. You really think an 11-year-old could live there all alone for two months?"

"She's not alone, she's got the dog," said Georgie.

Venice said, "That would make life harder, not easier. She'd have to feed the dog as well as herself. Anyway, someone would have noticed them by now."

I said, "Like who? No one goes in there. Even if someone did, the dog would hear them coming and she would have time to hide. There are loads of hiding places in that garden."

Georgie said, "Why don't we go back and check the place out?"

I looked at Venice. Venice looked at me. I could see she was about as keen on the idea as I was – which is to say, not keen at all.

On the other hand, that girl might need help. She ought to get those bites treated. But if she was really living rough, she might be afraid of hospitals, vets, or anyone who might ask awkward questions.

In the end Venice and I decided to go back. "Not you, Georgie," I said firmly. She was about to make a fuss, so I warned her about the dog which could be doing guard duty. Although he had been wounded, you could bet he still had a nasty bite.

The afternoon was dull, cold and grey, like the sluggish water of the canal. As I slid through the gap in the hedge, I felt myself shiver – not only from the cold. Were we being watched? Would I hear a sudden growl and feel sharp teeth locking on to my ankle?

"This is spooky," whispered Venice, as we slid between the leafless trees.

We avoided the open spaces, keeping to the side of the garden. There was a greenhouse, or rather the white bones of a greenhouse with most of the glass missing. In the vegetable garden, weeds grew almost head high. I couldn't imagine why anyone would want to live here, surrounded by ruin and decay.

The wash house door stood half open, with a drift of dead leaves against it. More dry leaves had blown into the room. I ventured inside and scuffled around in the corner where the bedding had been, but found nothing under the leaves except a stone floor. The store of apples had vanished from the window sill. There was no sign that anyone had ever been here.

"Happy now?" asked Venice.

I nodded. The girl could not be living here. She probably had a perfectly good home, with parents who would look after her, clean up her wound and fuss over the dog. She was not my problem.

"Let's go," said Venice, shivering slightly. "I don't like this place. It *is* haunted – I can feel it."

We hurried back through the bare winter trees. I kept wanting to look over my shoulder. But there was no one behind me, only the dark, empty windows of the deserted house.

The swimming coach had placed adverts in all the local schools: "Sandersfield Swimming Club needs *YOU!*" She wanted to attract some older members, but at first the only newcomers were yet more eager 10-year-olds.

Then, one day, half a dozen St Margaret's girls turned up. They were all boarders who had compulsory Games on Saturday mornings, but who hated hockey and lacrosse. For a trial period they were being permitted to swim instead.

Spotty Sam must have told his friends about them, because several Year 11 boys arrived the following week. At Sandersfield High, girls from St Margaret's had a reputation. They were all supposed to be:

a gorgeous.
b stinking rich.
c snobbish.
d desperate to meet boys.

The St Margaret's swimmers must have been a bit of a let down. They were no better than average-looking – in fact one was quite fat, as fat as I used to be. They certainly didn't look desperate to fling themselves at Sam and his friends.

But also, they weren't as snobby as I expected. In the swimming pool café, where I usually had a drink after training, they called me over to their table and we got introduced. "Amelia, Alice, Kate, Fiona, Loose..."

"Lucy," the fat girl protested. "Not Loose," but everyone ignored her.

"Hi, I'm Phoebe."

Then they started quizzing me about the Year 11 boys – especially Callum, the best-looking one. (So maybe they *were* desperate. Callum was only a Grade B/C.)

By the time their minibus arrived, I had got to know the girls quite well. I hoped they would carry on coming to the club. It was nice to have people my own age to talk to. Especially when one of them was fatter than me...

For years I had been used to fending off fat jokes and critical glances. For years I'd been "the fat one". Now Loose, or Lucy, was in that position, and I'd been moved up a place. The not-so-fat-one. The plump one, the chunky one.

Well, it was an improvement. What I longed for was the day when my size wasn't mentioned at all, because it would be nothing out of the ordinary. People would describe me by my hair or my face or my ingrowing toe nails or whatever. Maybe one day... one day I would simply look normal. Who could ask for more?

Chapter Twelve

Moulded

My church used to have a really good youth leader. I always enjoyed the Sunday night youth group meetings when Pete was in charge. But he moved on to work in an inner-city church. That left Becky running the youth group. I hate to say this, because she's quite a nice person – but as an organiser, she's rubbish. She couldn't run a bun fight in a bakery.

"Tonight I've got a video that you might like to see," she said in her mouse-like voice. "Anyone think that's a good idea?"

Hardly anyone heard her above the chatter, so Luke Evans thumped on the table. "Video! Yes or no?" he roared, and most people answered "Yes". (I really think Luke would do a better job than Becky, but there's one problem – he's only in Year 9.)

The video showed a factory where plates and things were made. A big machine squeezed clay into moulds, giving rows and rows of identical dishes. Then we saw a potter using an old-fashioned wheel. He used the same raw material – a lump of clay – but he shaped it skilfully by hand. If it went wrong, he squashed it down, started again, and worked on it until it was exactly how he wanted it. No two things he made were quite alike.

There was hardly any commentary, but I could guess what this was all about. God made us like the potter makes his pots – not identical copies, but unique individuals created with love and care.

Next came a series of images from adverts, all

showing beautiful girls. Although their expressions varied (sultry pout, beaming smile or arrogant stare), their faces were very similar. When the camera moved over a crowd of ordinary people, there was far more variety. Ugly and beautiful faces, young and old, black and white, with all shapes and sizes of eyebrow, nose and mouth.

Then we saw some of the things the advertisers were trying to sell — new cars, expensive clothes, exotic holidays. All this will make you happy! Aim for this and you'll be a success! You'll fit in with everyone else!

"Don't let the world squeeze you into its mould," said the voice-over. "Let God transform you and renew your mind."

A lively discussion followed the video. OK, so God made us all different, but is it wrong to want to look better? Should we ban all orthodontists, plastic surgeons, beauticians, hairdressers? Should Christians be noted for their ugliness?

"It's not just about beautiful and ugly, though," said my friend Sarah. "Being squeezed into a mould... that could mean other kinds of pressures. Wanting to be the same as your friends. Not being the odd one out..."

"Peer pressure, you mean?" said Becky.

"Yes. I sometimes feel as if God wants me to do something, or say something — but I'm afraid of what my friends will say. I don't want to look different and perhaps get laughed at."

Other people nodded in agreement. Becky said, "I think everyone gets that feeling sometimes. I know I do... and it was far worse when I was in my teens. So, what can we do about it?"

How to relieve peer pressure - some suggestions:

a Don't have any friends.
b Only have friends who are Christians – positive peer pressure.
c Become known for being slightly weird, but harmless.
d Fight back. Stand firm. Defend your principles, quoting 23 different Bible verses. (Then see a above.)
e Just give in, go with the flow, and become identical to everyone else. Does it really matter?

"Yes, it does matter," said Becky quite firmly (for Becky). "As Christians, our first priority should be to do what God wants. We mustn't let other people's opinions become more important than God's voice."

Luke said, "Sarah, what was the thing you didn't do because of what your friends might say?"

Sarah looked uncomfortable. "Well… there's a girl in my year at school who often gets picked on. She's overweight, and people tease her about it. At least, they would call it teasing. She would probably call it bullying."

"And you feel as if you ought to try and stop this?" asked Becky.

"I can't possibly stop it – not on my own. There's a whole gang of them, you see. If I say anything to upset them, they might start picking on me instead."

"You could mention it to a teacher, couldn't you?" someone else suggested.

Sarah said, "I tried that, but it didn't do any good. This is St Margaret's we're talking about. They'd never admit they have a bullying problem."

"Didn't the teacher do anything?"

"Sure. She gave the whole class a lecture about respecting people's differences and that kind of stuff. You can guess how much effect *that* had."

"Probably made things worse," I said. (Been there, done that, got the T-shirt.) "Does this girl have any friends?"

"Not really. I don't actually like her much myself," Sarah admitted. "She's so depressed all the time. But then I think, well, anyone would be depressed in that situation. And she's a boarder, so she's stuck with it 24/7."

We talked for a bit about what Sarah could do. I quoted what my mum always says... if you're not sure of the right thing to do, try to imagine how Jesus would act in the same situation.

"That's easy. Think of Zacchaeus," said Paul, who knows the Bible inside out (but then he is the son of the minister). "Jesus made friends with all the lonely people, the unpopular ones."

"Yes, and look what happened next," said Miranda. "The people who hated Zacchaeus started hating Jesus too."

Paul said, "But Jesus didn't care. He never worried about what people thought of him. All he cared about was doing the will of God, his father."

"I wish I was as strong as that," Sarah muttered. "But I'm not."

"None of us are," said Becky. "Not on our own, at least. Remember what it said on the video..."

After about six attempts, she managed to rewind it to the right place.

"Don't let the world squeeze you into its mould. Let God transform you and renew your mind."

"Romans chapter 12," Becky said. "What does that

actually mean… let God transform you?"

"Let him change you."

"Listen to him, obey him."

"God can shape us and mould us to what he wants us to be," said Paul.

"And what does he want us to be like?" asked Becky. "More beautiful? Cleverer? More popular? More successful?"

Luke said, "More like himself."

I whispered to Sarah, "The girl you were talking about – is her name Lucy?"

She looked startled. "Yes. How did you know?"

"Aha. Ve haf our spies effrywhere… She goes to my swimming club."

By now I had seen the way the St Margaret's girls treated Lucy. Some of them were really mean to her, making it plain that she wasn't part of their group. They laughed at her and made catty comments about her size. Sometimes they played stupid tricks on her – putting five sugars in her coffee, nicking her towel, hiding her bag while she was in the toilet. Childish, or what?

Lucy tried her best to ignore these little "jokes". Someone must have told her that if she didn't react at all, the teasing would stop. The trouble was this strategy wasn't working. Or maybe Lucy wasn't a very good actress… anyone could see how hurt she was.

I had tried to keep out of it. I had been equally friendly to all of them. But perhaps in future I should make an effort to be nicer to Lucy. It sounded as if she needed every friend she could get.

Chapter Thirteen

Keep practising

Although it was now December and the weather wasn't great, I carried on with my exercise programme. When there were no dogs to walk, I went out walking anyway – or even running. Yes! Amazingly, I could now run for several blocks without collapsing in a panting, red-faced, sweaty heap.

It was annoying that my weight had hardly changed. But the trousers I'd bought last summer were now too short in the leg and miles too big around the waist. So I was still growing and shrinking.

I was also getting fitter. In Games we sometimes had to do cross-country running, which I used to hate because I always finished hours after everyone else. (Our Games teacher is a total sadist who makes everyone complete the course unless they break both ankles.) I could hardly believe it when, this time, I managed to keep up with the field. OK, I was still last, but only by metres, not kilometres.

"Excellent, Phoebe," said Miss Marne. "You look as if you've lost some weight."

I couldn't answer – I had no breath at all. I had collapsed in a panting, red-faced, sweaty heap.

Other people began to notice the change in me. When Ellie and I went to Venice's house, her mum asked me if I'd been dieting.

"What's the secret, Phoebe? Do tell. I need to lose a few pounds, with Christmas coming up."

"*You* don't need to worry," I said. Fleur still looked as

slim as in the days when she had been a famous model.

"Oh, but I do, otherwise I wouldn't stay in shape. Which diet are you on? Food combining? The celery soup diet? High fibre? Low carbohydrate?"

"I haven't really been dieting at all," I said. "I just stopped eating snacks like biscuits and crisps, and started exercising. Oh, and I grew about three inches taller – that helped."

"You're lucky. You're so young," Fleur said enviously. "Not like me, getting old and past it, with cellulite and broken veins and laughter lines…".

I couldn't feel too sorry for her. Although she hated being over 40, she was still stunning to look at. She still made men stare at her as she walked down the street. And yet she wasn't happy with her appearance! Maybe no one ever is. Maybe, even if I got down to size 10, I wouldn't feel confident about my looks…

"But you look great," Ellie told Fleur, knowing this was what she needed to hear. "You don't look any older than 25."

Venice said, "Pretty soon I'm going to look older than my own mother."

"Oh no, darling, that won't happen. But people do sometimes think we're sisters, don't they?" Fleur looked as if she liked this idea… Venice hated it.

Changing the subject, Venice asked me if I'd heard from Pierre lately.

"Yes," I said. "We keep in touch by email. I even wrote a French email – I've found a website that does translation for you."

Ellie was interested. "This website – could it do my French homework?"

"It wouldn't get you very good marks," I said. "It only translates one word at a time, so it often gets things horribly wrong."

I had tested it by translating a phrase from English to French, then from French to German and back into English. The results were interesting. "I can't stand him – I hate his guts" came back as "I cannot hold it – I detest its entrails."

No wonder Pierre had been rude about my efforts to write French. Well, not rude exactly... just typically honest.

```
I think you must work harder,
Phoebe. You must learn the French
better inside your head. A computer
can't do this for you - you cannot
bring the computer when you visit
Paris.
```

It's such a shame that there's no instant way to learn a language – you just have to keep on practising, slowly getting better. Perhaps one day they'll invent a translating machine that you can carry around like a mobile phone. (And perhaps one day they'll come up with an instant slimming pill.) In the meantime, we simply have to do it the hard way.

At the weekend there was a swimming gala. Now that we had more members in my age group, I was free to concentrate on my best event, the breast stroke. Kate would swim freestyle, Amelia back stroke and Lucy butterfly. (Lucy wasn't brilliant at butterfly, but she was better than the rest of us.)

Our team was starting to look quite good. We occupied a large section of the poolside seats. Lucy was sitting by herself at the back – maybe this was my chance to be a bit more friendly.

Actually, I felt quite reluctant to sit next to her. People like Charlotte might make mean comments about Two Fat Ladies. And Lucy was so down in the mouth, I felt depressed just looking at her. Judging by her face, she didn't want to be here, so why had she agreed to come?

"Anyone sitting here?" I asked her.

"No." She couldn't manage to drag a smile onto her face.

Despite the lack of welcome, I sat down. "Is this the first time you've been to a gala?" I asked, and got a silent nod in reply. Oh dear... this could be hard work.

"It's only my second time," I admitted. "I was dead nervous at the last one. I kept thinking, what if I come last and everyone laughs at me?"

"That's exactly how I feel," Lucy muttered. "I wish I hadn't come – I feel sick."

"I bet Kate and Amelia feel just the same, except they're better at hiding it."

"You think so?" Lucy looked doubtfully at the other girls. They had found seats as close as possible to Callum, Sam and friends. Now they were talking rather loudly and laughing too much.

I said, "Either they're nervous or they're trying to impress the boys. Probably both."

That made Lucy smile. She seemed to decide that I might possibly be on her side.

"Those two will laugh at me whatever happens," she said, "whether I win or lose. So why should I care?"

"Girls 14 to 15, 100 metre butterfly," came the announcement.

"Good luck," I said.

I really hoped she would do well, to give her confidence a bit of a boost. But she came last, and returned looking even more despondent than before.

"See? I should never have come," she muttered.

"It was close." I tried to encourage her. "You only lost by a fraction of a second. Keep practising and you'll do better the next time."

"There isn't going to be a next time."

"Oh, but don't give up! Swimming is so good for you." I explained what it had done for me – how much fitter and healthier I felt.

"It's all right for you. You were never this fat."

"Yes I was. I used to be a size 20. Now I'm down to 16... well, most of the time. 18 on a bad day."

"Really? You used to be as fat as me?" She looked me up and down as if she couldn't believe it – which made me feel good. I decided I might actually like Lucy after all.

She started telling me how awful things were at school. The food was lousy, so she kept buying snacks from the shop even though she knew they were fattening. She had no friends. People picked on her for being fat and ugly, which made her depressed, and when she was depressed she ate even more.

I said, "If you hate school, can't you talk to your parents about it? Maybe you could move to a different school and things would get better..."

"I already tried that. I used to go to school in Marling, but I got picked on there as well. It's so unfair! I never have any friends!"

I could see she was what Mum calls a "Yes, but" person. Whatever advice you gave her, she would come up with a reason why it wouldn't work for her.

Lucy, you know you shouldn't eat so much junk food.

Yes, but the school food is so horrible.

You could spend your pocket money on fruit instead of sweets.

Yes, but the school shop doesn't sell fruit, only snacks.

You could do more exercise.

Yes, but I hate hockey and I'm no good at swimming.

You shouldn't complain so much. It drives people away.

Yes, but I can't help it. I'm so depressed! Nobody likes me...

It was a relief to hear my race being announced. I won the first heat quite easily and went through to the final. Could I do better than my bronze medal from the previous gala? I certainly felt fitter. I'd had a few more weeks to train...

"Come on, Phoebe! You can do it!" called Pauline.

I recognised the girl on the next starting block. At the last gala, she had won the gold, beating me by over a metre. Oh well... I could only do my best.

She was slightly ahead as I surfaced from the dive. All the way down the pool I fought to stay level with her. When we reached the turn we were neck and neck.

I'd been practising turns – this one was perfect. Surfacing, I realised the other girl was no longer in view. I was in the lead! But don't relax... keep going... find the strength for one last burst of speed...

I hung on the rail, feeling totally exhausted but full of triumph. I'd done it! I had won my first gold medal!

Wanting to share the wonderful moment, I looked over to where Lucy had been sitting. But her place was empty; she must have slipped off to get changed.

Hold on, though... what about the relay race? All four of us were supposed to be in it – Kate, Amelia, Lucy and me.

Pauline, our coach, called us together. "We've got a problem. Lucy's suddenly got a stomach ache, so she won't be able to swim in the 14 to 15 relay."

"Oh, terrific." Kate sounded angry. "Sudden stomach ache? She chickened out, you mean."

Amelia said, "She does this all the time... feels ill when she doesn't want to do something. But there's nothing wrong with her. She's just putting it on."

Pauline looked as if she might agree with this expert diagnosis. But she didn't say so. "Well, I can't force her to swim if she doesn't want to. So either we pull out of the relay, or one of you will have to swim two legs. Any volunteers?"

"But I'm useless at butterfly," I said.

"So am I. We all are," said Kate.

In the end, Kate agreed to swim twice. She did her best, but still lost us a lot of ground (or should that be water?). Then she had no energy left for her 50 metres of freestyle. We came in last by a long way.

No one could say if we would have done better with Lucy there. But we certainly couldn't have done any worse. And any points we might have gained would have increased our final total for the team. Two more points would have won us third place overall.

In the changing room, no one spoke to Lucy. I avoided her myself. Afterwards I felt rather guilty – suppose she really had felt ill? I had believed what Kate and Amelia said, even though I knew they didn't like Lucy. Why? Because I didn't like her much myself.

Befriending the lonely was easy to talk about, not so easy to do. Oh well... perhaps I would get better if I kept on practising.

Chapter Fourteen

The search

One Friday after school, Ellie and I were walking Boris, a powerful-looking bulldog. Actually, Boris wouldn't hurt a kitten. He was quite timid, afraid to walk past certain trees, and absolutely terrified of the door to the vet's surgery.

We went down Charles Street, on the opposite side from the vet's – and that was when I saw the girl. Even if I hadn't recognised her, I would have known that dog anywhere. It seemed he had been in another fight... a serious one. He lay limp in his owner's arms, looking half-dead.

"Look, Ellie," I said. "Over there – it's the girl I met that time when I was out with Rolf. And that's Matt, the dog who attacked him."

Ellie was interested. "Looks like he bit off a bit more than he could chew this time. I wonder what it was – a Rottweiler?"

The girl disappeared into the vet's place. It was rather odd, I thought, that she was alone. Whenever Ellie took her cat to the vet, her mum would go too. But perhaps the girl's family didn't like the dog and didn't care what happened to him.

Or perhaps she didn't have a family at all. I remembered my earlier suspicion that she was a runaway, living rough. But it was December, and the last few nights had been freezing cold. I hoped she had found a warmer place to sleep than that stone-floored shed at Hill House.

I was intrigued by her; I wanted to find out more.

"You go on," I said to Ellie. "Take Boris for his walk. I'll wait until she comes out, and follow her."

I went into a chemist's shop opposite and spent ages near the window, pretending to choose some make-up. When the shop assistant started giving me funny looks, I moved to the bookshop next door. The bookshop man didn't seem to mind people browsing, which was just as well, because it was almost an hour before the girl came out of the vet's.

The dog wasn't with her. Oh... perhaps he was so badly hurt that the vet had to put him down...

No, that couldn't be true, because the girl didn't look upset. More likely the vet had operated on Matt and was keeping him in overnight to make sure he was all right.

The girl went off down Charles Street. I slipped out of the shop and went after her. It was getting dark by now; in the town centre, all the Christmas lights were on. But she walked right down the High Street without even glancing at the brightly-decorated shops.

She made for the Coldfield Estate on the edge of town. Was that where she lived? It was a scruffy area, but then the girl herself was quite scruffy. Her hair was longer and more untidy than ever. Her jacket would have looked like an Oxfam shop reject, even without the stains of dog's blood.

As the streets grew emptier, I kept further back. But it was pretty dark and I was certain she hadn't seen me. Up one road, down another, she sauntered along, going nowhere in particular. Then she turned in at a gate and rang the doorbell of a house.

A light went on, and a man answered the door. It looked as if the girl was asking him a question and he was giving her directions. She came down the path and walked past a few more houses. She almost rang another doorbell, but a loud barking sound made her change her mind. Instead, she went to the house next door, which was all in darkness.

This time no one answered her knock. The girl gave a quick glance up and down the road – just in time, I dodged behind a tree. When I looked out again, I couldn't see her. She must have gone round the side of the house.

What on earth was she up to? Was she searching for an empty house where she could break in and steal things? I hurried along the street until I could see down the passage between the houses. But there was no sign of her.

Rather nervously, I tiptoed down the dark passage. I could hear furious barking from the house on my left, which almost drowned out another sound... the crash of breaking glass.

I ran round the corner – and there she was. She had smashed a pane of glass in the back door. Now she was reaching inside, trying to undo a bolt or a key.

"Hey! Stop!" I shouted.

Her reaction was instant. I was blocking the exit to the street, so she ran the other way, across the back garden. Agile as a squirrel, she swung herself over the fence and disappeared into the woods beyond.

I ran after her, but stopped at the fence. The woods were pitch black – she could be anywhere. I had lost her.

Maybe she actually lived out there. Boys often built shelters in those woods – good for hiding in, but not much use against the cold winter wind. Or maybe she lived with the travellers, who were back in town, camping on the waste ground by the old factories. (Mrs Gillespie had warned everyone to keep their doors locked.)

I turned back towards the house. There was a gaping hole in the door – anyone could reach the key. While I was wondering what to do about it, I heard an angry voice.

"Oi, you! What are you doing? Get out of there!"

A middle-aged woman was looking over the fence on the right. I tried to explain that I hadn't done anything, but I could see she didn't believe a word I said.

"Go on, get out of there! I'll call the cops!" she shouted.

"Fine. Call them," I said. "Somebody ought to report this. Here – you can use my mobile."

Still looking at me with distrust, she took the phone and rang the police. Then we had to wait for ages before they sent someone round. Rather grudgingly, the woman invited me inside her house, but she didn't leave me alone for a second.

When the police came, I described the girl in as much detail as I could. "And another thing – she's got a dog that she left at the vet's in Charles Street. She would have to give them her address, wouldn't she? You could catch her when she goes back to collect the dog."

As I said it, a thought occurred to me. "Vets cost money. I bet that's why she tried to break in – to steal some cash to pay the bill."

"It's possible," said one of the policemen. "It's also possible this could be linked to a series of thefts. Have you heard about the Pension Day robberies?"

"*Heard* about them? My own family got robbed."

"Well, one of the later victims caught a glimpse of the thief, and gave us a description that ties in with yours. Young girl, longish brown hair, quick on her feet…"

"But it can't be the same one," the neighbour objected. "I mean, it's not pension day today."

Was she stupid, or what? "She can't wait till pension day," I said. "She needs the money now, to get her dog back. So she just decided to steal from any old house, hoping there would be some cash there. I saw her knocking on doors, looking for an empty house. She's probably somewhere else in town by now, trying the same trick."

The policemen thanked us for our help and got ready to leave. "What about the hole in the back door?" I asked.

"Don't worry, I'll keep an eye on the place until the Browns come home," said the neighbour. "Not that they've got much that's worth nicking."

Before I set off home, I rang Ellie to tell her what had happened. She suggested we could meet at the vet's to see if we could find out anything more.

Mrs Black, the vet's assistant, was about to lock up the surgery. But Ellie knew her quite well, being a regular customer with her cat. When she explained what was going on, Mrs Black looked worried. "Yes, I know the girl you mean. We've patched up that dog of hers a couple of times. She always comes in on her own, and pays for the treatment in cash, which seems a bit odd. I mean, you don't expect a child to carry that much money on her..."

"Stolen money," I said.

"Did she give you her name and address?" asked Ellie.

Mrs Black looked up the records. "Kylie Smith, 83 Beech Lane."

"Kylie Smith? I bet that's not the name she was born with," I said.

"My dad lives in Beech Lane," said Ellie, "and I'm sure it doesn't go up to number 83."

We were no further forward. Walking home, I felt discouraged. Then Ellie suddenly said, "We could try the Internet."

"Oh sure. Do a search for what exactly? Long brown hair, freckles, dogs, robbery?"

"No. Missing children. If you're right, and she's a runaway, her details might be on some website somewhere..."

It was worth a try. Our first search turned up loads of sites from all over the world. Even when we restricted it to the UK, there was a lot of information to sift through. It was depressing and rather frightening. Who were all these people who had been reported missing? What had happened to them... would they ever be found?

We looked at dozens of photos, until my memory of the girl's face began to get confused. "This is hopeless," I said.

"Just a few more, then we'll stop."

Another two photos, and another two, and then –

"There she is!" I cried. "It's her!"

Chapter Fifteen

Another theft

There were a few details with the photograph.

NAME: Holly Baker.
AGE: 12.
LAST SEEN: 3 July, Wetherbury, Somerset.
HEIGHT: 5 feet 1 inch.
BUILD: Slim.
EYES: Brown.
HAIR: Brown.

The girl in the photo was very similar to our mystery girl, except that her hair was much shorter. She had the same freckles and the same stubborn mouth. "I'm not going to smile for the camera, and *you* can't make me do it, so tough."

I wondered why she had run away… what sort of home she had come from. Were her parents cruel to her? Was she an orphan, perhaps?

Another mystery: what had brought her here from Somerset and kept her here for so long? I had seen her first in September, quite soon after our house was robbed. That was almost three months ago. I wondered where she had been living for all that time and what she had been doing, apart from stealing, that is.

There was a contact number to ring, but it was now almost 9 pm on a Friday night. No one answered my call.

"If it's an office number, there won't be anyone there until Monday morning," said Ellie.

I was dying to find out more, but she was right. I would probably have to wait until Monday.

Next morning I went off to the swimming club, wondering if Lucy would turn up. She was there, looking unhappy. "What's the matter?" I asked her.

"The others are still being mean to me because of the gala. I want to give up swimming and do hockey instead, but Miss Wells said I have to wait until next term. It's so unfair!"

Lucy was very slow to get changed. Most of us were ready to swim while she was still in her changing cubicle. Creeping up, Amelia reached a hand under the door and pulled something out – Lucy's swimsuit. It must have been lying on the floor.

"Hey! Give that back!" came a shout from inside the cubicle.

"Why?" said Amelia. "You're not exactly going to need it, Loose. After the first five minutes, I expect you'll sneak off with a headache or a stomach ache or something."

"Or a pain in the neck," said Kate, and everyone laughed.

Lucy appeared, half undressed. She seemed to have given up on her policy of "ignore them and they'll go away". Actually, she couldn't ignore them this time, unless she was prepared to swim in her underwear.

"Give it to me," she said, making a grab for it. Amelia threw it over her head to Alice, who chucked it to Kate.

"Piggy in the middle!" cried Charlotte, joining in.

Alice said, "Elephant in the middle, don't you mean?"

It was a most unequal contest – four against one, with a crowd of younger girls looking on and laughing. Lucy looked as if she might burst into tears.

"Oh, give it back to her," I said as casually as I could. "You know how Pauline hates it when people arrive late."

"Or leave early," said Kate, tossing the swimsuit to Charlotte.

Obviously they weren't going to listen to me. So I leapt for the swimsuit as it flew past, and made a lucky catch. I gave it to Lucy, who looked pathetically grateful.

Four hostile faces turned towards me.

"Don't tell me you're on *her* side," said Alice.

"Fatties stick together," Charlotte giggled, and Amelia said, "Yeah. Fat girls of the world unite! You have nothing to lose but your chains... I mean chins."

"Rather unfair to lump the two of them together like that," said Kate. "Lucy may be the size of a house, but Phoebe's only the size of a bungalow."

There's not much you can do when it's four against one. I smiled at them as sweetly as I could. "So it's true what they say... girls who wear size 10 and under have a mental age to match."

While they were working that one out, I headed for the poolside. (Lucy by now was back in her cubicle, where I hoped she had the sense to keep everything well away from the door.)

I tried to put those stupid comments out of my mind and concentrate on my training. As this would be the last session before the Christmas holidays, I made it a good one. Pauline was pleased with me. At the end of the session she called me over.

"You've made amazing progress in the last three months, Phoebe. Well done! Keep it up, and you might end up swimming for the county!"

She made it sound like winning Olympic gold. I didn't care about swimming for the county, but I did intend to keep on getting fitter. In the shower, I looked down at myself and noticed something new. My feet! I never used to be able to see them when I stood up straight – my big fat stomach always got in the way.

I dried myself, feeling rather pleased. Pauline was right: I had made amazing progress. Keep on like this, and in a few months no one would be able to call me fat...

I had been last in the shower queue, so I was still getting changed when the trouble started. I should explain that during Club sessions the pool was closed to non-members. Some people had become rather careless about their things – instead of spending 20p on a locker, they just left their belongings in the cubicles.

Now they were finding out how foolish that was. I heard cries of dismay as people discovered their money was missing. A few of the younger girls had lost the money they'd been given to spend in the café. Kate's purse was missing, with more than £20 in it, and so was Amelia's, with £10. Nothing had been taken except cash; other valuables like mobiles and watches were still there.

This was exactly like the Pension Day robberies. Only cash taken... by a thief who slipped in and out without anyone noticing... had the mystery girl struck again?

There was a commotion outside my cubicle. "Hey, Loose," I heard Amelia shout. "Where d'you think you're going?"

"To the café," said Lucy, sounding surprised.

"She was sneaking off again," cried Kate. "Now why would she do that?"

"She stole the money! She's a thief!" Charlotte yelled.

"I didn't," said Lucy.

"I bet she did," said Amelia. "Trying to get back at me for nicking her swimsuit."

Lucy said indignantly, "I never touched your money. How could I? I've been swimming for the last hour, like everyone else."

"Yes, but you were the last person to get into the pool. The last one out of the changing room," said Kate.

"That wasn't my fault! It was because you lot stole my swimsuit!" Lucy was getting upset again. Unfortunately, some people took this as a sign of guilt.

"Look inside her bag," said Alice.

"No! Let go! Leave me alone!"

I could go out there and say something in Lucy's defence. I could tell the St Margaret's girls about the local robberies, which might be news to them. But would it make any difference? Probably not, I told myself.

I really didn't want to get involved. The easiest thing would be to keep my door shut and simply ignore what was going on. After all, nothing I could say would make them be nice to Lucy – they would just start hating me.

"If you've got nothing to hide, why not prove it?" I heard Kate say.

"Yeah. Show us what you've got in that bag, why don't you?" cried Charlotte.

"Because you'll start chucking my things around again," Lucy gasped. "Get off me! Stop it!"

I felt sorry for her – of course I did. But not sorry enough to go out there and show that I was on her side... to risk being insulted and mocked. I didn't want to be her Fat Friend. I wanted to be one of the normal people, not the freaks.

"Got it!" someone shouted triumphantly. "Here, see how much money she's put away."

I heard coins being tipped on to a bench. "That's *my* money! Put it back!" Lucy cried. There was a scuffling sound, as if she was trying to break free from arms that held her back.

"There's not much here," said Kate, disappointed. "Only a couple of pounds. She must have hidden the rest in her pocket or somewhere. Hold on to her for a minute."

"Pull her hair if she tries to move," said Charlotte.

Without a sound, I packed my bag. I would wait until all this was over, then slip quietly away…

More scuffling noises – then a cry of pain. Someone swore loudly. A bench went over with a crash, and people screamed…

Then there was a horrified silence.

I opened my door. Lucy was lying on the floor outside, quite motionless. She looked as if she had fallen over backwards, banging her head on the tiles.

"That wasn't my fault," said Kate. "I never even touched her."

"Nor did I. It was an accident," said Amelia. "She slipped on the wet floor."

"Is she dead?" Charlotte whispered.

Some of the girls looked rather guilty. But not as guilty as I felt.

Chapter Sixteen

Caught by the net

Lucy wasn't dead – just unconscious. But she still had not come round by the time the ambulance carried her off to hospital.

I thought of the dreadful things that a bad fall could do... brain damage, total paralysis... And I could have stopped it from happening. Well, perhaps not stopped it, but at least I could have tried. I had been too cowardly, too worried about what everyone else would think of me...

Pauline went to the hospital, after phoning the school to tell them what had happened. The St Margaret's girls had to wait for their minibus, which was running late. Now was my chance to say what I should have said before – that Lucy wasn't a thief. There wasn't much I could do to help her, but at least I could clear her name.

The other girls didn't believe me at first. Then I had a bright idea. "If I'm right, the thief could have been caught on CCTV."

"Don't be stupid," said Amelia. "As if they'd have CCTV in the changing room!"

"There's a camera in the corridor outside," I pointed out. "Why don't we ask at Reception?"

With all the commotion about Lucy, no one had got round to reporting the stolen money. When we told the receptionist, she called the manager, and he replayed the CCTV tapes from the previous hour.

First there was a deserted corridor. Then suddenly, there she was – the mystery girl, racing along it at high speed. The manager pressed a button and she slowed to normal walking pace. She strolled into the changing room as if she had every right to be there.

"But how did she get into the building?" the receptionist asked. "She never came past the front desk, I swear she didn't."

The view from a different camera answered that question. It showed the back of the building, where there was a fire door, normally kept shut. The cook from the café came out with a bag of rubbish, propping the door open so that she could get back indoors. In the ten seconds while she walked to the bins, a small figure slipped around the door and disappeared inside.

"Well I never," said the receptionist.

"You'd better check the till," the manager told her.

"I've been sitting right here ever since we opened," she said. All the same, she did check the money in the till, as if the thief might be skilful enough to nick it from under her nose.

"Now do you believe me?" I asked Amelia and her friends.

"All right. There's no need to go on and on," said Kate.

I was angry now. "You never really thought Lucy was a thief – did you? It was just another excuse for having a go at her."

A couple of the girls looked uncomfortable. But Alice muttered, "She deserved it."

"*Deserved* it? Why? Just because she looks different, just because she's fat, she deserves having you make her life a misery?" I took a deep breath. "I suppose you think she's some kind of freak, and you're the normal ones. Well, if normal means being like you lot – thanks, but no thanks. I'd rather be one of the freaks."

I marched out. There. I'd said my bit. Probably none of them would ever speak to me again, which was no great loss.

But it was all too late to help Lucy.

I desperately wanted to talk to someone about what had happened. But Mum and Dad had gone Christmas shopping; Ellie was at a rehearsal for the school play, and Venice wasn't answering her phone. Then I thought of my friend Sarah from the youth group. She already knew Lucy from school – she would understand the situation.

I rang her and told her about it. "Oh, how awful," she said. "Is Lucy going to be all right?"

"I don't know. I called the hospital, but they wouldn't tell me much because I'm not a relative."

She tried to reassure me. "Most likely she'll be fine. My brother once fell out of a tree and fractured his skull..."

"Yes, and look what that did to him," I said. "You're supposed to be making me feel better here, not worse."

"Oh, Phoebe – don't feel bad. If anyone feels guilty, it ought to be Amelia and her gang. None of it was your fault."

"Yes it was," I said miserably. "I could have said something that might have stopped them picking on her. But I didn't want to go against the crowd. And now I keep thinking about that video at youth group. You know... don't let the world squeeze you into its mould? That's exactly what happened today. I messed up totally."

She was silent for a moment. Then she said, "Remember the start of the video – the man making pottery? When it didn't turn out like he wanted, he didn't throw away that lump of clay. He just started again, and worked on it until it came out right."

"What are you telling me? I remind you of a lump of clay?"

"No, idiot. I'm telling you God doesn't give up on us when we go wrong. He's always ready to start again – if we let him."

Start again… OK.

I'm really sorry, God, I messed things up… forgive me. And please change me, make me more like you want me to be… And help Lucy to get better.

Handmade pottery takes time. It can't be done instantly. And shaping people takes time – a lifetime. God must be very patient, is all I can say.

Feeling a bit better, I made myself some lunch. Georgie was at a friend's house, and Mum and Dad wouldn't be back for ages. They were taking Josh to see Father Christmas at Marling shopping centre. (Complete waste of time and money, because everyone already knew what Josh wanted for Christmas… lots and lots of cars.)

Checking my emails, I found Pierre had replied to mine from the previous day. I had told him all about the mystery girl – it was the sort of thing that interested him.

```
Dear Phoebe,
   I think I am better detective than
you. A detective must use every piece
of information. I have looked up the
name of this Holly Baker on the
Internet. Please look at www.wether-
burynews.co.uk, in the page for the
8th July, also the 29th September. Is
this the same person?
```

At once I looked at the website he mentioned. It belonged to a weekly newspaper. As well as the latest news ("COUNCIL APPROVES NEW CAR PARK"), there was a brief summary of the main stories from previous issues.

12-YEAR-OLD GIRL GOES MISSING – this was the main item for 8 July.

"Schoolgirl Holly Baker was reported missing from the foster home where she had been living for two months following the death of her mother. She is believed to have run away. She was last seen on 3 July at Wetherbury coach station, boarding a London-bound coach."

Then there was a brief description of the girl, and a quote from her foster mother... "I've no idea why she ran away. She always seemed perfectly happy here."

Happy? When her mother had died not long before? That sounded rather odd to me. I looked up the other date Pierre had mentioned.

"FOSTER PARENTS ARRESTED... John Farley (38) and his wife Tricia (35), foster parents for five years, were arrested on 25 September, accused of cruelty to children in their care. Police are trying to trace all the children who passed through their hands, in particular Holly Baker (12), who was reported missing in July."

That must be why she ran away. Her mother had died, and she had been put with foster parents who treated her badly. Poor kid!

When I started looking for the girl, it was because I was angry – she'd stolen our money. Then I became curious rather than angry. Now I actually felt sorry for her; I wanted to help her if I could.

But maybe she didn't need my help. After all she had managed to survive for months on her own. (Not totally on her own, of course – there was the dog. Where had she found it? Perhaps it was a homeless stray, like herself.)

It was amazing that she hadn't been noticed by anyone official. People must have seen her around town — perhaps they assumed she was one of the travellers who came and went. And her story had never been on the national news. It was in her local paper, but Sandersfield was a long way from Wetherbury. (Was that the reason she chose to come here? If so, why stop at Sandersfield? The Outer Hebrides would be even further away.)

I printed off all the information. Clever old Pierre! I ought to thank him... Then I saw he'd emailed me again.

> Dear Phoebe,
> I think it's a good idea to go back to the Hill House, where you have met this girl. Perhaps she lives there. What do you think?

I thought it was a lousy idea. I didn't like the place, and anyway we had checked it over already, on the day of the dog fight.

But that was weeks ago. Even if no one had been living there at the time, things might have changed... Maybe I should take another look.

I rang Ellie, who was home by now. She was keen to be involved.

"I could bring a dog with me," she suggested. "The one I'm supposed to be walking today has a really good nose – she could be our sniffer dog."

"Brilliant idea," I said. The dog would be safe from attack by Matt because he was still at the vet's.

Just as we were getting ready to go, Venice rang. I told her what we were doing. "Oh, can I come too?" she asked eagerly.

"Sure." Safety in numbers, I thought to myself.

Chapter Seventeen

Secret Lair

Daisy was not a pretty-looking animal, but Ellie was right about her nose. She wanted to sniff at every blade of grass along the canal towpath. When we came to the hole in the fence she got very excited.

"Perhaps she can smell that other dog," said Ellie.

Daisy led us through the garden with her nose to the ground. I expected her to make for the door to the wash house, but she ignored it, heading for the side of the main building. Here she sniffed around a small, boarded-up window set at ground level – a cellar window, by the look of it.

Was it possible that the girl had managed to get inside the house? I looked more closely at the window's board.

"Hey, look at this!"

The corners of the board were splintered and broken, as if they had been forced away from the wall. Just one nail still held it loosely in place. You could swivel it up and over, revealing the cellar window – or rather the window frame. It looked as if someone had smashed the glass, then carefully removed the broken fragments.

There was a drop of about a metre and a half to the floor below. An upturned wooden crate was placed there to act as a step.

"Wow! She got into the house!" said Venice admiringly. "No wonder she gave up sleeping in that wash house place."

Ellie said, "We don't know it was her. It could be anyone."

"Anyone with a dog," I said, because Daisy was sniffing hopefully with her head right inside the window. She was obviously dying to explore further. If Pierre had been there, he wouldn't have hesitated for a second. But the three of us were more cowardly – or more sensible.

"It looks awfully dark in there," said Venice.

"We could come back another time, and bring a torch," I suggested.

Then Ellie said, "Actually, I've got a torch on my key ring. It's only a little one…"

We looked at each other. No one wanted to go in there… but no one wanted to chicken out.

"Let's do it," I said. "But if anyone gets scared, we all come out, right?"

None of us (except Daisy) was keen to go in first. In the end Ellie volunteered. I passed the dog down to her – luckily Daisy was the size of a Yorkshire terrier, not a St Bernard. Then Venice and I followed her.

Ellie flashed the tiny torch around, showing a stone-paved cellar with a low ceiling. Apart from a heap of coal, it was empty. Moving slowly forwards, I felt something touch my face, as soft as a ghostly finger. I gave a yelp of fright.

"What's the matter?" Ellie cried.

"Nothing. Only a cobweb on my face."

"*Only* a cobweb?" said Venice, alarmed. "You know I hate spiders."

"Shhh. Come on," said Ellie. The dog was tugging her towards a flight of steps.

At the top of the stairs, a door opened onto a hallway almost as dark as the cellar. Thin slivers of light showed through gaps in the window boards. The torch beam slid over dark brown paintwork, faded velvet curtains, and a curving staircase going up into the dark. There were four doors, all closed.

"Which way now?" Venice whispered.

I held Daisy's lead as she sniffed around the hall, sneezing when the dust went up her nose. One particular door seemed to interest her. Very gently, I turned the handle.

The door opened on darkness – darkness and warmth. (The hallway and cellar felt colder than the garden.) Silently Ellie passed me the torch, and I let Daisy pull me into the room.

It was a big, old-fashioned kitchen. The warmth came from a coal-burning stove which looked as old as the house. A heap of rugs and blankets lay next to the stove, as if for bedding. Someone was definitely living here. There were dirty plates on the table, clothes piled on a chair, candles stuck into saucers… Daisy sniffed at a dog basket and a feeding bowl, already licked clean.

I shone the torch around – then suddenly I froze. That heap of rugs by the stove was moving.

Daisy began to nose around it. A voice groaned, "Go away, Matt. Leave me alone. Go back to sleep."

Then a face emerged, pale in the torchlight – a freckled face half hidden by long, untidy hair. No doubt about it… I had found Holly Baker.

I half expected her to leap up and run. But she sat up slowly, shielding her eyes against the torchlight. Her voice was slurred with sleep.

"Hey, what's going on? What are you doing in my room?"

"*Your* room? I like that," said Venice.

"We were exploring the place," I said, keeping my voice as friendly as I could. If we made an enemy of the girl, we would never find out anything. "Do you live here, then?"

"What's it got to do with you?" she said aggressively. "Who are you, anyway?"

"Just girls like you." I shone the torch on each of our faces in turn.

She didn't like us all staring down at her. Pushing the blankets aside, she got to her feet, rather unsteadily. She was fully dressed and the room was warm, but I noticed she was shivering. Perhaps she wasn't feeling too good.

"Are you OK?" I asked her.

"Why shouldn't I be?" she snapped.

"Well, you were sound asleep in the middle of the afternoon."

"I sleep when I feel like it," she said. Her face was sullen.

She went over to the table in the middle of the room. After several attempts, she managed to strike a match and light a candle. Then she sat down hurriedly, as if she felt faint.

The candle flame lit the room better than Ellie's torch, although darkness still lurked in the corners. The floor was covered in greasy brown matting; the walls were dusty and cobwebbed. There was a stone sink, full of dirty pans, and an old wooden dresser. Apart from a portable TV and a stack of tinned food, everything was ancient, shabby and faded.

"Nice place you've got here," said Ellie.

"Yeah, well now you've seen it you can get out," said the girl. She clearly hated us being there, but it was three against one – she couldn't force us to go.

Venice said, "We've got as much right to be here as you have."

"That's not true! I found this place. I got here first."

"So? That doesn't make it yours," said Ellie. "But then you've made a habit of that, haven't you? Taking things that don't belong to you."

I nudged her with my elbow, trying to make her keep quiet. But the girl had hardly noticed what she'd said. She was staring at Venice and me.

"I've seen you before," she said accusingly.

My heart sank. But it was OK – she wasn't talking about her burglary attempt the night before.

"Out there," she said, "in the garden. Your dog had a go at Matt."

"Other way round, you mean," said Venice. "That dog of yours is a raving lunatic. He'll get himself killed if he keeps on attacking German shepherds."

"How's he doing – your dog?" I asked her.

"He's not too good. He got in another fight," she admitted.

Looking as if she suddenly felt hot, she took off her jumper. She winced with pain as she moved her left arm. There was a rough bandage around her wrist.

"Did you get bitten?" Ellie asked.

"Might have done. What's it to do with you?"

"You ought to go and see a doctor, Holly," I said.

That got her attention all right. "Hey, how do you know my name? Who told you?"

"Nobody told me. You're on the Internet – look." I took the printout from my pocket and unfolded it to show her photo. She stared at it, fascinated.

"It is you, isn't it? And take a look at this." I showed her the news item about her foster parents. She read it carefully in the flickering candlelight. A slow smile appeared on her face.

"They deserve it," she said. "They deserve to rot in jail for years."

"Why? What did they do?" asked Venice.

"You really want to know? OK, I'll tell you."

The candle flame made dark hollows around her eyes. I knew she was only 12, but her face looked hard and old. She was probably tougher than any of us.

"Sit down," she said. "And don't stare at me like that."

She began to tell us her story.

Chapter Eighteen

Nowhere else to go

Holly said, "When I was a kid, I lived in the country. There was just me and my mum. I don't know where my dad is – he went off years ago. Good riddance, Mum said. But we were OK, just the two of us..."

She stopped talking, as if she didn't want to move on from that time in her life – the time when she was happy. There was a silence.

"But something happened to your mum?" I said.

"Yeah. She got killed. Run over by a drunk driver." There was no emotion in her voice at all.

"How awful," Ellie breathed.

"Mum always said if anything happened to her, I was to go to my nan's. She said my dad was a waste of space, but his mum – my nan – was all right, and she would look after me. And she made me learn the address. 83 Beech Lane, Sandersfield."

I looked at Ellie. That was the address which Holly had given to the vet – the address which didn't exist.

"After Mum..." Her voice faltered. "After Mum died, I got taken into care. I told the social workers about my nan, and they tried to get in touch with her. But she'd moved away – at least that's what they told me. They said it would take time to find her. So I got put with foster parents."

"The ones who got arrested a few months ago?"

"Yeah. At first I thought they were OK. They acted all nice in front of the social worker. But when she went away, I found out what they were really like."

She hugged herself tightly. She was shivering again.

"They were worst with the little kids," she said. "There was this boy called Jamie – he used to wet the bed. He was only 3, he couldn't help it, but John used to whack him every time, and Trish rubbed his face in the wet sheets. Jamie was terrified. After a while he used to wet himself whenever they came near him."

"Did they ever hit you?" I asked.

"No. I reckon they thought the bruises might get noticed at school. But if I didn't do what they said, I got no food. Other times they locked me up in the attic. They were horrible. They shouldn't have been allowed near kids – not in a million years."

"But why didn't you tell someone what was going on?" asked Ellie.

"Who was I supposed to tell? I didn't know anybody in Wetherbury. I'd had to move away from home, and change schools, and everything. Anyway, it would be useless. I would only get moved somewhere else that might be even worse."

"So you ran away?"

"Yeah. The social worker was never going to find my nan – she couldn't even be bothered to try. So I decided to look for her myself. One day I took some money from Trish's bag. When they thought I was at school, I got on a coach to London, then a train to Sandersfield. Dead easy, it was."

But then things began to go wrong...

She said, "I found Beech Lane all right – but there wasn't any number 83. The lane was a dead end. There was a huge great motorway where my nan's house ought to be."

She must mean the Sandersfield bypass, which had been built about ten years ago.

"I asked this woman, and she said a whole row of houses got knocked down when the road was built. And no, she didn't know where the people moved to. So that was it. I couldn't find my nan."

"But there must be ways of finding out where she went to," I said. "The council would know, or the post office, or somebody. She didn't just vanish into thin air."

Holly gave me a scornful look. "What's going to happen if I go to the council and start asking questions? They'll start asking *me* questions, that's what. Then they'll find out who I am and send me back. And I don't want to go back there – not ever."

"You wouldn't have to go back to those foster parents, though," said Ellie. "They're in prison."

"Who's to say the next lot would be any better? Anyway, I can't. They wouldn't let me keep Matt in a foster home. They'd take him away. I'm not having that!"

I asked her where she had found the dog. She said it happened the day after she arrived in Sandersfield. With nowhere else to go, she had spent the night in the woods on the edge of town. Cold and hungry, she awoke to the sound of a dog squealing in pain.

"I saw these two boys with a puppy, tormenting him... kicking him around. So I stole him off them," she said proudly. "I followed them home and saw where they shut him in the shed. They didn't deserve to own a dog! Specially not a dog like Matt. He may not look like much but he's dead clever. He helped me find this place."

She looked around the dingy room as if it was a palace. "And it's ours! You're not taking it away from us!" she said fiercely.

"But you won't be able to live here for ever," said Ellie. "Some day the lawyers will decide who owns this house, and the people will want to move in, or sell the place..."

Holly looked alarmed for a moment. Then she said, "Who cares? If they do, I'll move on somewhere else. Somewhere even better!"

Her face was flushed. It was warm in the room, but not warm enough to make me sweat like Holly. She wiped her forehead with her sleeve.

I asked her, "What will happen if you get ill? You don't actually look one hundred per cent at the moment."

"I'm all right," she said irritably. "I just need a drink." She stood up, swayed slightly and sat down again.

"Let me get it," I said, heading for the sink.

"Not there, the water's turned off. Pass me a bottle."

There were some bottles of water beside the tinned food on the shelf. I gave her one, and she drank from it thirstily. All her supplies must have been bought with stolen money, I realised. If she went on living here, she would have to keep stealing just to stay alive.

The same thought occurred to Ellie. She said, "You can't keep on like this. It isn't right, what you're doing, taking money off old people and kids."

"But I need it more than what they do," said Holly. "They're all right. They can get more money the next week. All they have to do is go and ask for it at the post office. I can't do that, so I have to steal it."

"It's still wrong," said Venice.

"What do you know about it?" Holly cried. "You with your designer clothes and fancy trainers? You probably spend more in a day than I do in a week. I bet you don't know what it feels like to be hungry, do you? If you were desperate, you'd steal things too!"

"Perhaps we would," I said. "But you don't have to be desperate. There's no need for you to live like this. There are people who would help you, and you could live in a proper home again."

"With running water and baths and things," Ellie put in. (It was pretty obvious that Holly hadn't had a bath for quite some time.)

"You sound exactly like the social workers," Holly said bitterly. "Be a good girl, we'll look after you, they said... and then they handed me over to John and Trish."

"But most foster parents aren't like that," said Venice.

"Oh yeah? And how many foster homes have you ever been in?" Holly sneered.

"Well, none, but..."

"Thanks, but no thanks. I don't need anyone looking after me. I can take care of myself."

Try a new angle, I thought. "If you want to get back at John and Trish, you should go to the police. They need evidence—"

It was a mistake. I shouldn't have even mentioned the subject.

"The police!" She stared at me, horrified. "I'm not going near no police. Are you crazy?"

"Look, they won't lock you up, if that's what you're worried about..."

"Get out. Get out of here!" she cried. "I'll set my dog on you if you don't. Here, Matt! See 'em off!" She looked around desperately.

"Your dog isn't here. He's at the vet's," Ellie reminded her.

"Get out of here or I'll kill you!" Her eyes were wild and feverish. She got up, staggered across the room and pulled a drawer open. When she turned round she was holding a kitchen knife. "I mean it. Just get out!"

The three of us backed towards the door, with Daisy barking like mad.

"It's OK. We're going," I said.

I pulled the kitchen door shut behind me.

We scurried across the hall and down the cellar steps. At the bottom I stopped to listen, but there was no sound of footsteps following.

"That girl is a nutter," said Ellie.

"Either that or ill," I said. "She looked feverish to me."

"What do we do now?" asked Venice. "Tell the police?"

"Yeah. She's not safe loose," said Ellie.

I was still listening. Suddenly, right overhead, there was a loud crash, like furniture toppling over.

"What was that?" Venice gasped.

"Sounds like she's barricading herself in," said Ellie.

But there were no more sounds of movement from above. All at once I remembered Lucy falling over in the changing room. The sudden noise, the silence after it, the body lying there motionless...

"Maybe we should make sure she's all right," I said.

"You're joking," said Venice, heading towards the cellar window. "Come on, let's get out of here."

"No, wait a minute," I said.

Still there was silence. I couldn't get the thought of Lucy out of my mind. Lucy had people around her to call for an ambulance. But if Holly had hurt herself, she would have no one to help... no one at all.

"We should go back," I said.

"No way," said Ellie. "She's probably hiding behind the door with that knife in her hand."

"Let's get outside and ring 999," said Venice. "Call the police and an ambulance as well, if you like. Oh come on, Phoebe! We're wasting time!"

Seeing me still hesitate, Ellie grabbed me by the arm. "She doesn't need us – she said so. She can take care of herself."

"That doesn't seem to include washing herself,"

said Venice. "Phew! She does smell."

"She's weird. Leave her alone," said Ellie.

I allowed Ellie to pull me towards the window. Venice scrambled out, and Ellie lifted the dog up to ground level, then followed her. We were close to safety… so why did I feel so terrible?

Because it was happening again – that's why. I was going along with other people instead of doing what I knew was right.

Don't let the world squeeze you into its mould. Let God transform you and renew your mind…

I stopped abruptly, halfway out of the window. "What's the matter?" asked Ellie. "Oh no – don't tell me you've got stuck."

I said, "I'm going back in. I've got this feeling… I just want to check if she's OK."

Ellie and Venice looked at each other as if I was totally crazy.

"You're on your own, then," said Ellie.

"Yeah. I wouldn't go in there again – not for anything," Venice said.

I slid down to the floor, checking that I still had Ellie's torch.

"Oh, Phoebe… don't do it," Ellie begged me. "Remember that knife!"

"Why don't you wait for the police? Look, I'm calling them now," said Venice.

I turned away from them. I walked across the cellar and up the steps into the dark, silent house.

Chapter Nineteen

Casualty

Cautiously I knocked on the kitchen door. Was Ellie right? Was the mad girl lurking behind the door with a knife?

There wasn't a sound. "It's only me," I called. "Can I come in?"

Still no answer. Then I noticed the smell… a faint, smouldering, burning smell. I pushed the door open, and the smell grew much stronger. I saw the glow of flames, far brighter than a candle.

"Fire!" I screamed, praying that the others would hear me. "Help!"

Holly lay on the floor near the table. She must have dropped the candle, or knocked it over. The matting on the floor was smouldering in an ever-widening circle, and flames licked at the heap of rugs and blankets.

Call the fire brigade. No – get her out first. Oh, help! Please help me, God!

I ran over to Holly. The fire was still a metre away from her. I tried to drag her away from it, but she was a dead weight, impossible to move.

"Holly! Holly, wake up!"

No response. Looking around frantically, I saw a bottle of Evian on the shelf, grabbed it and splashed water onto her face. She groaned. Her eyes flickered open.

I emptied the bottle of water on the nearest flames, which hissed and sent up a cloud of black smoke.

"Holly, come on! We've got to get out of here!"

She tried to get up, then collapsed again, coughing

from the smoke. Across the room, a curtain burst into flames. There wasn't time to go for help. If I left her here she would die.

The back door was the nearest way out – but it would be locked and boarded up. Same with the front door. The only way out was the way we came in.

"Holly, get up. You've got to help me. I can't lift you, not on my own…"

"Phoebe!" Someone was calling my name.

"In here," I gasped. "Quickly."

Through the smoke, I could just make out two faces – Venice and Ellie. Oh, thank you. Thank you, God.

Between the three of us, we managed to lift Holly. We got her out of the kitchen and shut the door on the flames. That might give us an extra minute or two.

"We'll never manage to get her out through the cellar," said Ellie.

"Call the fire brigade," I panted.

"We already did. How long will they take?"

"There must be another way out," said Venice, looking around. "Give me the torch."

She vanished through one of the doors leading off the hallway. Half a minute later she was back. "There are some French windows. I opened one. Boarded up on the outside – we'll have to break out."

We lifted and dragged Holly through the door, shutting it behind us. Venice shone the torch around. A living room with heavy old furniture – piano, ancient radio, marble fireplace. Nothing here that would help us break through the boarding outside the French windows.

Ellie picked up a heavy vase and hurled it against the wood. The vase smashed into pieces.

I realised Holly was trying to say something. "An axe… over there…" she croaked.

Venice shone the torch towards the fireplace. It looked as if Holly had been trying to split logs on the hearth. And yes – the axe was still there.

I grabbed it and swung it as hard as I could against the wooden boarding. Painful shocks went through my hands. I tried again. At last, with a splintering noise, the axe head went through the wood. Peering through the small gap I'd made, I saw a flashing blue light at the gateway.

"Help!" I yelled at the top of my voice.

Two policemen came running. Within a minute or two, they had chopped a large hole in the boarding and released us from our prison. We were safe – all four of us.

But what about poor Daisy? "Where's the dog?" I said, panicking.

"Tied to a tree in the back garden," said Ellie, and she ran to get her.

Daisy was fine. She sniffed our smoky clothes, then decided the ambulance was more interesting, and the fire engine even better.

By now the driveway of Hill House looked like a scene from *Casualty*. The fire-fighters unreeled their hoses and dragged them into the house. The paramedics got Holly onto a stretcher. I thought she might object – then I saw she was unconscious again.

We all had to go to hospital, to be checked for smoke inhalation. Ellie, Venice and I were OK, but Holly had breathed in more smoke than we had. She also had a very high temperature. The doctor said it was probably caused by infection in the dog bite on her arm.

"Will she be all right?" I asked anxiously.

"I'm sure she'll be fine. But we'll keep her in until we

get that temperature down. Can you tell me her name and address? We need to contact her family."

I hesitated. "She hasn't got any family... except her dog. And her address is the house that caught fire."

"What? You mean she's been living there on her own?"

Although Holly would probably hate us for it, we told him the whole story. He looked grave.

"I'll have to get in touch with the Social Services people," he said. "She can't go on living like that."

"She doesn't think much of social workers," Ellie warned him. "Don't be too surprised if she runs away again. She's quite tough — thinks she can take care of herself. But she can't, not really."

"Yes, I can see that."

I said, "What she really needs is to find her nan. Is there any way you could help her do that?"

He thought for a moment. "If this story gets into the paper, her grandmother might read it and get in touch. That is, if she still lives in the area. Ten years is a long time."

"It's worth a try, though. Isn't it?"

"Of course," he said. "I know a reporter on the *News*. Leave it with me."

Chapter Twenty

Fresh start

Two days later Holly's picture was on the front page of the *Sandersfield News*. The following day, she was in the national papers. A reporter had talked to her in hospital and got the whole story.

The newspapers made her out to be a poor little helpless child – not at all like the Holly I knew. They didn't mention her criminal career, although the police knew all about it by now. They focused on her mother's death, her dreadful foster parents and her quest to find her grandmother. There was even a photo of Matt, still recovering from his wounds. (Mrs Black at the vet's was looking after him.)

Ellie, Venice and I went to visit Holly. We took the newspapers to show her, but she'd already seen most of them.

"Famous, I am," she said, pointing to the row of Get Well cards on her locker. "People I've never heard of sent all that lot. Some of them even sent money to pay the vet's bill."

She looked extremely happy, sitting up in her hospital bed, with lots of people to look after her. But she wouldn't be able to stay there for ever.

"Any news of your nan?" Ellie asked her.

The smile vanished from her face. "Not yet. I dunno… she might be dead. Or left the country. Or else she doesn't want to know me."

I asked her when she would be coming out of hospital.

"Tomorrow or the next day, they said. I don't know

where they'll send me after that. But I already told them – if I don't like it, I'm not staying around."

A nurse came towards us. "Holly, there are two more people here to see you. I've asked them to wait for a few minutes because we don't allow—"

"Who are they?" Holly interrupted.

"Family, they said."

"It's OK. We were just going," said Venice.

We passed the visitors in the corridor – a grey-haired woman and a man a bit younger than my dad.

"Do you think that was Holly's nan?" I whispered.

Venice said, "Oh, I hope so. And the man – he looked awfully like Holly. He couldn't be her dad, could he?"

He *was* her dad, as we found out next day.

"Mum always made him out to be really bad," said Holly. "But he's not. I reckon Mum hated him after they split up, so she wouldn't let him come and visit me. It was like she was punishing him. After a while he stopped trying to see me. But he never forgot me – he still has my photo in his wallet."

"What's going to happen now?" I asked.

"I'm going to live with them. With my dad and my nan." She looked really excited. "They live in Yorkshire, out in the country… Matt will love it. There's only one problem."

"They've already got a dog?" Ellie guessed.

"They've got three. All bigger than Matt."

"Perhaps he'll finally learn not to fight," Venice said.

And perhaps Holly would learn to be part of a family again, to stop stealing, to be less fiercely independent… She would be making a fresh start. I really hoped things would work out for her.

"Keep in touch," I said. "Let us know how you get on."

Someone else making a fresh start was Lucy. I had tried to visit her in hospital, only to find that she'd already been sent home. She had recovered from her fall, but she didn't want to go back to St Margaret's. Her parents were looking at different schools nearer to their home.

Would she get on any better at another school? Or would she still be the same old Lucy?

I thought of her quite often, feeling guilty about my failure to help her.

"I feel bad too," said Sarah. "I didn't help her either. But my dad says, don't carry those guilt feelings around with you. Say sorry to God and to the person you hurt, then start all over again with a clean sheet."

"But I can't say sorry to Lucy. I'll probably never see her again."

Sarah said, "What I do is, whenever she comes into my mind, I say a prayer for her. Feeling guilty won't help her, but praying might. And next time I'm in a situation like that, I'll try to handle it better."

"Yeah. Try to do what God wants – not what other people want."

I had actually managed to do that once already, when I went to help Holly. Venice and Ellie tried to persuade me not to go, but I ignored them. And the weird thing was that they changed their minds and followed me. (Just as well they did, or I might not be here now.)

So it's possible. One person *can* go against the tide. Sometimes, just one person can turn the tide and make it flow the other way.

It's almost Christmas, and I've hardly done any shopping yet – there's been too much going on. I'll have to join the frantic rush of last-minute shoppers buying perfume and chocolates and CDs and socks. It's such a shame I can't get people what they really want…

Perfect Christmas presents for:

Mum: chef, butler and maid to take care of
             Christmas dinner.
Dad: three months off work.
Georgie: £1000 to spend in a week.
Josh: real car to drive around in.
Ellie: boyfriend, grade A, six foot three.
Venice: boyfriend, grade A, lovely French accent.

And me… what do I want? For years, it was easy to answer that question. I wanted to be thinner. That would solve all my problems, I thought.

Well, now I am thinner. I'm around halfway to my ideal shape, according to those depressing charts in slimming magazines. So am I halfway to being gorgeous, fashionable, confident, admired by everyone?

No. I'm still the same old Phoebe. (A bit healthier and fitter, that's all.)

> … But that is good. I like you as the same old Phoebe. Please don't become a girl such as Julie, who think that everyone must love her because she is so beautiful. Become yourself, Phoebe. You are unique.

I'd better watch that Pierre. He must have been taking lessons from super-smooth Michel. Any day now he'll murmur, "Phoebe. What a beautiful name." (Pity you can't exactly murmur via email.)

But he's right. I am unique. So is he – so is everyone. We're all different, the way God made us. I may not be perfect, but then, God hasn't finished with me yet.

I don't want to be a clone of the latest fashion models. I don't want to be exactly the same as all my friends. I don't want to be moulded by adverts, peer pressure, TV, other people's opinions. I want to be what God wants me to be, unique and special.

Oh help... look at the time! Got to go. Got to rush around buying socks and perfume and chocolates and CDs, like everyone else. And I only have a couple of hours before the shops shut. Happy Christmas!

If you've enjoyed this book, look out for three more great books about Phoebe!

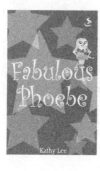

Me and my friend Ellie have a system for grading boys – like GCSEs.

A: Absolutely Adorable.
B: Better than most.
C: Could be OK, if…
D: Don't bother.
E: Excruciating.
F: Friend of Frankenstein.

The problem is, A-grade boys expect to go out with A-grade girls. (You know – gorgeous face, good figure, skin without a single spot. Brain cells an optional extra.) I'm not, if I'm honest, any higher than a C. Could be OK. Could be OK, if…? If I was thinner.

On top of that I'm trying to work out what the creepy Bird Woman is up to and talk to God about it all. And then there's the Awful Babysitting Incident. I don't even want to think about that…

ISBN 1 85999 678 7

Phoebe's Fortune

Reasons why I can't have more pocket money according to Mum and Dad:

1 Because money can't buy happiness (true, but it does mean you can be miserable in comfort).

2 Because Dad is a teacher, not a multi-millionaire.

3 Because when he was my age he only got 15p a year, blah blah blah.

4 Because if I got extra money, my sister would have to get some too, or it wouldn't be fair.

5 Because if I'm so desperate, why don't I get a paper round or something?

6 Because it's time I learned that money doesn't grow on trees (if only!).

Money makes people do crazy things, but how far will Phoebe and Ellie go to get some extra cash?

ISBN 1 85999 700 7

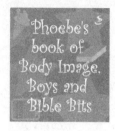

Mum asks me, "If everyone else jumped over a cliff, would you do it too?"

A: Yes, if it looked like they were having a good time on the way down.
B: Yes, because I'd be so lonely without any friends left.
C: No, because my mum would make me wait until I'm older.

Get great advice from fabulous Phoebe (and the Bible!) in this essential survival book!

ISBN 1 85999 663 9

You can buy these books at your local Christian bookshop
or online at www.scriptureunion.org.uk/publishing
or call Mail Order direct
08450 706 006